THEN HE HAPPENED

CLAUDIA BURGOA

Then He Happened

Sign up for my newsletter *to receive* updates about upcoming books and exclusive *excerpts.*

www.clauidayburgoa.com

 Created with Vellum

Also By Claudia Burgoa

Standalones

Maybe Later

My One Despair

Knight of Wands

My One Regret

Found

Fervent

Flawed

Until I Fall

Finding My Reason

Christmas in Kentbury

Chaotic Love Duet

Begin with You

Back to You

Unexpected Series

Uncharted

Uncut

Undefeated

Unlike Any Other

Decker the Halls

For Sebastien and all the amazing people who have worked with him throughout the years.
For my family and my readers

"So, I love you because the entire universe conspired to help me find you."

— Paulo Coelho, The Alchemist

Prologue

Jason

Eight Years Ago...

"YOU CAN'T STAY HERE," Jack, my brother, says as he looks down at me. "We've got to move on."

I sit on the steps of the altar, staring at the envelope burning a hole in my hand—the one she served me with, ensuring a life sentence of agony and despair.

For a moment I wonder the meaning of Jack's words. Is he talking about the garden? Or the moment? I snort. Who cares, I can't even breathe.

For fuck's sake, my world just shattered, and he wants me to move. I can't feel my legs.

How can I move on?

I can hear the advice coming from everyone who just witnessed the devastation of Jason Spearman's world. Mom was the first one to hit me with her *wise words*.

"Love can last forever if you're with the right person," she said after I fell to the ground, defeated.

What did she mean by that?

I *am* in love with the right person—my soulmate. At least, that's what we've said to each other. Or were her declamations of love useless words meant to enchant me? Meant to make me believe that her love for me was absolute?

It doesn't matter anymore. She's gone.

And now here I am, broken without a clue on what to do next.

My error was to fall in love.

As if my dad could hear my thoughts, he says, "Loving someone is never a mistake."

He pats my shoulder and leaves to do some damage control. There's nothing they can do that will repair what happened today. My heart is breaking. Blood oozes from my wound, not that anyone can see what's happening to me.

My throat is thick, I'm having a hard time swallowing—or breathing.

I loosen my bowtie, gasping for air. My throat is thick.

"I should've known," I say out loud.

Neither one of my brothers says a word. They remain close enough in case I need them but giving me the space I crave. The rawness of this moment shreds my gut, and I am left questioning everything. Wondering what I'm supposed to do now?

"How will I survive?" I tighten the grip of the fucking paper I haven't read.

"By living the best life that you can," Alex, my younger brother, says. "You slap that bitch by showing her this didn't affect you. There's life after her. You are Jason fucking Spearman."

But how will I survive?

1

Jason

THE SOFT MELODY of a piano follows me around like a lounge singer. She plays me something jovial to shake the stage fright out of me.

The air is as thick as smog caught in a smoker's exhale, but I can make out the faint outlines of the audience somewhere in front of me.

Hesitantly, I sway to the tune the piano titters out, both of us awkward and stiff from years of neglect.

Someone in the first few rows wolf whistles to encourage me. I put a little more swagger into it—like my drama teacher used to tell us in high school put your soul into your hips and make love to the world.

Yeah, in hindsight that was fucked up.

But the audience eats my lame moves up with a silver spoon. A sound comes out of my throat, a lot like the shit I used to sing. It's like being a different person.

It feels like being alive.

The piano gets to an accelerando, and I run out of shits to give. I belt out my baritone blues of being lovelorn and exhausted, of *counting down the days until my life makes sense again... is really truly mine.*

I get a standing ovation and almost forget my stage turned into a rundown wedding altar halfway through my set. The cheering fades as the piano's sweet loving melts into ear-piercing blares—

MY CELL PHONE WAKES ME AT ASS O'CLOCK IN THE MORNING. Cold sweat trickles down my spine as I reach toward the nightstand for my phone to check who is calling me.

Great, it's my attorney.

"Go for Spearman," I say, the lump in my throat clogging my airway and my fucking hollow chest.

Fuck, it was just a dream. Yet, my heart still pounds hard as if it just re-lived through the agonizing moment when my entire life...

"Finally. I've been trying to reach you for the past couple of hours," my lawyer, Fitz Everhart, says, ignoring that he lives two hours ahead of me.

He should've learned to fuck off this early in the morning by now. I sigh, squinting as my eyes adjust to the dim blue light coming from the hallway.

Maybe I should call him before I go to bed. Wake him up at three a.m. his time and see how he likes it.

With an enormous effort, I heave myself out of bed. I fish a pair of underwear out of the neglected laundry pile next to my closet before I head to the living room. Maybe I should hire a housekeeper. That's a subject for another time.

"Well, you got me," I say finally, rubbing my eyes. "Where's the fire?"

"I just sent you a new investment proposal. Have you decided about the one from last week?" he asks.

I groan in response. It's too fucking early for this.

"Look, I don't have a problem going through the proposals, but you have to give me an answer right away after I send you the details."

This is one of the reasons why I hired Everhart and his team. They go through all the proposals, contracts, and documents. They save me time by combing through this shit and spotting potential investments.

Since I sold my tech startup five years ago, I went with the only job in the world left for rich, soulless, *boring* dickbags—venture capitalist. Aside from the terrible networking events and wading through piles of shit ideas, it pays well.

Theoretically, it leaves me plenty of time to live my life. Nowadays, most of the ideas that actually get to me are profitable. They have lots of potential.

"I take it you're going to say no," Fitz implies.

"They want more than money," I argue. "I don't have time to hold anyone's hand right now."

"Makes sense," he says. "Well, I'm off to disappoint yet another person and add that you're only looking to *invest*—at the moment—into your requirements. You don't babysit or teach. In that way, you'll only get the proposals that make sense for you."

"Thanks," I say before hanging up.

Trudging back to my bedroom, I open the shutters, and the sun illuminates my room. That's when I see her.

The blonde I hooked up with last night never left. She rolls onto her stomach. She's still naked, eyeing me like meat, ready for another round.

"Well, it's been nice..." I pause, was it, Brittany or Lauren. "Umm, Lisa," I lie politely.

And by the stink eye she gives me I know I fucked up her name, but it's too early in the morning to remember my own name, let alone a piece of ass that should already be gone.

She flashes a fake smile as she says, "It's Lina."

Well, close enough, I think.

"You're kicking me out?" she says incredulously. "What happened to breakfast?"

"Who said anything about breakfast?" I sputter.

And who eats breakfast this early? I look at the time. Well, seven isn't that early as I thought but fuck if I don't need a cup of coffee.

"We could spend the morning together," she says suggestively.

Together?

What do people even do this early in the morning?

Turn on "Morning Joe" or some other corny show and talk about what? Gossip? Their opinions and what to cook? Share the same half cold cup of coffee with some lazily thrown together eggs and talk about what they're doing that day?

Who'd even like that quiet domesticity? *You did once, asshole.*

I shake my head while gathering her clothes.

"I don't know if you recall," I say with the same fake calm voice I used the summer I worked nights at a call center in Tuscaloosa back when I was in college. "But I *told* you that I had an early morning meeting. Staying over was your call."

I toss her clothes on her lap... her underwear may have *accidentally* hit her square on the nose. Not that it fucking matters at this point if she blacklists me online or some shit like that. If I hurry, maybe my assistant won't see her.

I don't bring people to my apartment, especially hookups. I hear a snort inside my head.

Valid, I only do hookups.

But honestly, I know better than inviting women into my apartment. They think sleeping over is an invitation to settle in and never leave.

I can appreciate a good fuck and decent conversation at two a.m. about docks in Amsterdam or "what do you think the Grand Canyon looks like right now?" But no one's ever interested in enjoying the moment.

They size me up while I'm flirting and decide I have something to give them. No one cares about who I am beyond their *Sex and the City* fantasy. I'd be insulted if I weren't so fucking tired.

"We had a good time," she says.

"It was fun," I admit.

It would've been more fun if you used your mouth as much as I used mine.

"Why don't we go one more round?" she asks with a pout.

I usually fuck once, and I leave—or in this case, she leaves. That's how it's supposed to work. This is what I get for asking her if she wanted to come over instead of sucking it up and going across town to her place.

We met at my downstairs neighbors' party so that also made wanting to go to a random apartment in Thornton impossible.

"You know what they say about too much of a good thing," I offer politely.

She scowls, moving the covers to offer glimpses of her body. When that doesn't entice me, she makes sure to offer her bare breasts, and open her legs wide, exposing her bare pussy.

Classy. I wonder where she picked up that party trick.

"You're a fucking asshole," she says like a mind reader. "I've heard of you in my circles. Jason Spearman, famous playboy and cold-hearted fucker."

"The one and only," I say, smirking. "Now do me a huge solid and get the fuck out of my room."

"I'm taking a shower," she mutters while heading toward the bathroom.

She stops right in front of me, pressing her breasts into my side.

"Unless you want me to stay for one last round," she attempts one more time.

She's really on my last nerve. I have things to do. And my assistant will kill me if she finds a naked woman in my house.

"Out," I repeat.

"What's wrong with you?" she screams this time. "I was hot enough last night and now I'm nothing to you?"

"Good morning, boss," Josselyn, my assistant walks into my bedroom, handing me coffee. "Great, we picked up a souvenir from last night's rendezvous."

"Jossie," I groan.

"You're an arrogant son of a bitch," Lyn? Liza? says storming almost naked out of my apartment.

Josselyn follows her with those bright amber eyes of hers and glares at me.

"Pretend you didn't see anything." I shut my eyes and try to concentrate on the sweet nothings the caffeine in this coffee is whispering.

After a couple of sips, I open my eyes to see her giving me a lopsided smile and a pat on the shoulder. "If I find you half-naked with a guest one more time, I'm quitting. Get ready. We have a lot of work to do."

2

Jason

FOR THE LAST couple of years, I've been helping my brother, Jack, with his company. At first, it was just with his clients. He's not what we would call a "people person," or "friendly," or "gives enough shits to have manners sometimes."

That's where I come in. I'm like his spokesperson or his professional wingman—swooping in to seal the deal and make him look like an empathetic billionaire.

He has a lot of rules when it comes to working for him.

Said rules have come in handy with my own clients and business deals. But regardless, there's still a little thing called common sense. And common sense says if I want people to trust me, I should probably not look like a womanizer while trying to close a deal.

My public image starts and ends with the shit that comes out of my mouth—including whatever my breath happens to smell like the morning after putting it to good use. Breath mints come in handy to remedy that.

Jossie would argue more than she probably needs to. But like I said, my mouth needs to be in top form. Which also means my version of small talk leaves out or ignores phrases like "What do you have planned after our meeting?"

Tonight, I've been pretty patient and discreet while having a business dinner. Even when there's a bombshell redhead by the bar with legs for days. I've only snuck a glance in her direction when I'm sure no one's looking. So exactly three times.

But hey, my research is as thorough as it is brief.

"I think we're set," Mr. Smith, my soon-to-be new business associate says, finishing his drink. "Please, have your lawyer send me the contract."

"You'll have it first thing in the morning," I say as I offer him a handshake. "It's a pleasure having you on board."

"By the way," Mr. Smith adds. "Let's meet to talk to about your brother's company soon. I heard he's going public."

I smile blankly. There's no reason to tell him that it's just another fucking rumor. My brother doesn't like to share. I walk Mr. Smith toward the exit where I shake his hand one more time, pat his shoulder, and watch him as he leaves.

I sigh when he's out of sight. Biggest fucking deal of the year and it went smoothly. I hope. We'll see if that holds up after he looks over the contract.

Jason Spearman: Send the Smith contract. He's on board.

Fitz Everhart: It's almost midnight.

Jason Spearman: Oops, I didn't notice. Goodnight.

I grin after I hit send and put away my phone. I head back toward the bar to go talk up that redhead who's been driving me crazy for the past couple of hours. I want a taste of her.

She leans forward when I get to her. Her palms rest on the wood bar, as a bartender sets a martini glass in front of her — two olives held by a toothpick float in the clear liquid.

"Evening," I say to no one in particular and then signal the bartender. "Give me your top shelf scotch on the rocks."

I give the redhead a subtle smile.

"Hey there," she says, a hint of a grin shows on her plump lips. "I was wondering how long it was going to take you to come and join me."

I slide onto the stool next to her, finally looking at her. Her emerald eyes stare at me hungrily. I'm interested enough that despite the blatant invitation I can see in her eyes, an invitation that would normally diminish her appeal, it doesn't turn me off.

Once the bartender serves my drink, I raise my glass to her in a silent toast, then I toss it back in one swallow. She flashes a smile, following suit but only taking a sip of her drink. I can appreciate that.

"You waited a long time while," I state, signaling the bartender for another drink. "I feel like I owe you something."

She licks her lips, takes her purse with her, and motions toward the back of the restaurant. "My place is near." She dangles a pair of keys. "Let me go and freshen up before we head out."

I tap my second glass of scotch. "I'll be waiting."

As she saunters away, I watch her luscious curves. My gaze stops when I spot a table close to the bar where an older couple is getting ready to leave.

He's helping her with her coat. I wonder how long they've been together. If they've always been this happy. If they ever ripped each other apart so bad they didn't come back together quite the same way.

I wonder if he ever came home to an empty house and whether or not he wondered if she'd ever come back to him.

What was it about her that made him believe that love exists?

"Ready?" Red says, standing right beside me. I have no idea when she got back or how long I've been staring at these people.

"Have been since the moment I saw you," I say, not really to her. But if she hears and assumes I mean her.

Who am I to spoil her fun?

Her eyes crinkle.

This is the part where she says something charming and I think, *hey, maybe she's something special.* Until I'm on a bed somewhere balls deep in her tight pussy wondering what I should have for lunch tomorrow.

When did sex get so tedious?

I look at the old couple again. After eight fucking years, it finally sinks in. I don't think I ever had the kind of relationship that outlasts a marriage with Greta.

We Spearmans are fucking unlucky when it comes to love. Greta made sure I didn't break that tradition. But thank fuck, I didn't have to go any farther than the altar she left me on.

3

Jason

"WHAT THE EVER-LOVING fuck happened to your furniture?" I ask when I walk into my brother's penthouse.

Jack's apartment used to ooze filthy-rich-business-mogul with more bare surfaces and black and white exteriors than the fucking Antarctic.

But for the past few months, every time I walk in here, it's like a progress photo on *Extreme Makeover "Whipped" Edition*.

It looks like a painting from the 40s was hit by a semi-truck of cat toys.

"Did your couch get eaten by the ghost of Christmas yikes?" I ask. I swear next time I show up, I'll be tripping over trains or blocks or whatever kids play with each other now. I shudder.

"Ramen and Sushi scratched the couches. Emmeline used that as an excuse to replace the living room," he says.

"I'm so sorry *he* did this to you," I lament to the memory of his bachelor pad.

He groans next to me, but I don't give a fuck. We used to be so alike, and now, he's another poor sap lost to the futility of settling down.

Where's my wingman when I need him?

Nesting, with some petite, curvy, snarling woman who has him hypnotized like a roadside attraction.

"I thought she wasn't moving in," I say.

Speak of the devil, Emmeline, Jack's girlfriend, walks in laughing. I wish I could say that I hate her, but she's not terrible. I'd go as far to say she's funny and kind, and socially aware in ways that make up for my brother's ineptitude.

"Good morning, Jason," she says with a bright tone that should be illegal. "To answer your question, no, we aren't living together."

"Sure you aren't," I say sarcastically. "Your furballs are taking over the penthouse."

"Like me, my kittens like to stay overnight," she says as she smirks at me. "Often."

"*Our* kittens," Jack says and then takes her into his arms and kisses her deeply.

Because of course he would. Obviously, they live in a movie where the side character, me, doesn't mind awkwardly standing there while they swap spit.

"Any day now," I hum.

"We're looking for a house," Jack says when they pull away. "When we find it, you'll be the first one to receive the news that we moved in together. She stays nightly because I'm kind of irresistible."

"So, *I'm* irresistible?" I ask Emmeline jokingly.

It is fun driving her crazy because that drives Jack crazy. That way, everyone's annoyed. I'm judicious that way.

She gives me a once over and shakes her head. "You two barely look alike. Your hair is lighter, your eyes are too for that matter, and you're shorter."

"By half an inch," I protest. "And I'm stronger than him." I flex and puff my chest for dramatic effect.

She waves at me dismissively. "You'll find your other half one day, Jason. Stop pestering me."

"Aw, come on, where's the fun Em with unending patience and a good sense of humor? We have fun here, remember?"

In all fairness, I may be pushing my luck. We may or may not have met because I tried to catcall her to piss off my brother. Boy did she rip me a new one after that.

She shrugs. "If you say so."

Yep, I'm definitely pushing my luck.

I could be less of a playful dick, but ever since I left San Francisco to be closer to Jack a year ago, they're the only family I see regularly. I have to capitalize on who I've got for as long as I've got.

So, if that means Em is eternally unamused by my bullshit, that's fine. As long as I keep getting invited to brunch.

"Coffee or latte?" Em asks from the kitchen, pulling me out of my thoughts.

"Espresso?" I ask hopefully.

She nods. "I heard you had a sleepover this week."

Fuck. Josselyn. She can't keep her mouth shut.

"You can't prove anything," I say defensively.

Em rolls her eyes. "Assistants talk, Jason. I just happen to get the 4-1-1 because I'm a fun boss."

"I need a new assistant," I complain.

"What you *need* is to get your act together," Emmeline says and looks over at Jack who's glaring at her.

See? That's what I'm talking about. They have their dumb, secret love language that I get shut out of, and it's only a matter of time before they start using their eyebrows to pick movies without me.

"Fine," she finally says to Jack. "I'll keep my opinions to myself. He can do whatever he wants with his life."

I restrain myself from groaning audibly. This is how it's been since they started dating. They're so bored in their happy ending they keep meddling in my life. There's nothing too big, or too small, in my life for them to want to change.

Well, it's Em who does it.

Some days, I wonder if she's just speaking for Jack? Why the fuck do they even care?

It's not like I tell them to stop fucking around the office.

It feels like a punch in the stomach, seeing how in sync they are. I'm glad my brother found someone who loves him. He deserves it after that fucking bitch who broke his spirit.

In fact, seeing them together makes me think coupling isn't as terrible as I make it sound. But then I remind myself that that's not who I am. And if I ever have reason to doubt that, I just recall the day I was left at the altar.

Fuck. I run a hand through my hair. I need a week away from their lovefest with someone exponentially more fun—or some people like that.

"Speaking of which." I clear my throat. "Can I borrow the house in Steamboat?"

Emmeline sets a platter of fruit on the table and looks at me shaking her head.

"Stop judging me," I say. "My body, my choices."

"Em," Jack says, shaking his head.

She mimes zipping her lips before sitting down. I'm impressed that she keeps quiet.

And she does. Until halfway through brunch when she just has to say—

"I'm just saying that if you continue with the string of meaningless hookups, you'll never find what you need."

Jack snorts, and I roll my eyes.

She can't keep her opinions to herself, can she?

"Almost ten years ago, this guy was telling me to live, and now his better half is telling me to stop." I wave my hand around. "Make up your minds, people. I'm happy. Take it or leave it."

"Keep telling yourself that," she insists.

So what if sometimes I wonder what it'd be like to find a woman who makes me grin like an idiot, the way Em does with Jack? It doesn't matter.

Been there, done that, got the t-shirt.

Emmeline is the exception to the Spearman rule. I'm fine just the way my life is.

I look at both of them, rub my chest, and sigh.

Yep, I'm fine. Who needs this?

4

Eileen

THE WOMAN'S mouth keeps moving. I tuned out a while ago... but I can't stop focusing on how weird her lips smack together. They aren't paying me enough for this. I'm ready to jump out the damn window into a garbage truck.

I swear, I spend thirty minutes during every session just listening to her rant about one thing or another. Listen, I love my job. It's just some of the parents of my patients... not so much.

"Working with teens and adults with special needs is rewarding," they said.

"You'll love everything about it," they lied.

No one warned me about the guardians who think they know everything.

"...You're doing it wrong," she finally gets to her point. "There's a better brand of therapeutic tape."

She walks to her coffee table and returns with the most expensive brand of tape on the market. I sigh.

"They use this in the Olympics," she explains, shoving the tape in my face. "What you're using isn't right and, according to the YouTube channel, you should be applying it from top to bottom."

I don't get paid enough to deal with parents like her. How is it that I work for a woman who lives in a high-end neighborhood and can afford to spend more money on magazines than I spend on groceries?

If I wanted to work with assholes like her, I'd be in a private practice.

"Are you listening to me?" she asks, as her flesh turns a red crimson as her anger and frustration grows. The vein on her temple is about to burst. Her green eyes are on me. "I'll be calling your supervisor about this."

I roll my eyes before staring her down. I'm ten weeks past done with her bullshit. "It's not about the tape. It's all about how you *apply* it. Let me explain to you again how it's done."

She picks up her phone and turns on the camera. "I'll be recording it. But I think you're wrong. Are you sure you're a trained professional?"

No, I just printed the credentials of my fucking hundred-thousand-dollar college degree from some website. I just throw money to a tuition loan company for fun.

Does she honestly think just anyone can get a job as a therapist?

I look around the living room—of the second floor of her fucking *mansion*—and say, "Are you sure you can't afford private therapy?"

She scrunches her nose and looks me over weirdly before she says, "I'm ready."

Well, I'm glad we understand each other, lady.

I begin to apply the tape on her son's back to retrain his posture. Jim is a sweet guy. He's almost twenty and is Autistic. I wish there were more resources for him, or that she would spend a little more money helping him.

Regardless, I just hate that she's always judging me while I work.

Rumor has it that she has run off at least seven therapists. No one wants to deal with her. The only reason I'm here is because I need the money. If I had the luxury of choosing my own hours, I'd be somewhere else.

"This isn't the way that the guy in the YouTube video does it," she says as I finish.

"Let's try this way first and see how that works," I suggest tightly.

I'm not going to give her my damn credentials. I have a doctorate in physical therapy. I can't deal with her constant condescension, but I also can't burn this bridge any time soon, or possibly ever.

"Next week, I think we should go to the park," I say. "Work on his coordination."

"You're an *at-home* therapist," she argues.

"I understand that. But unfortunately, you don't have the equipment that I need. The stuff I have in my car is for small children."

She rolls her eyes. What is she? Twelve? "Fine, but I'll be with you. He can't be alone with a stranger."

"Of course," I say, grabbing my tote bag and wave at her son, Jim, waiting for him to wave back. "See you next week, Jimbo."

He gives me a wide smile and walks toward his room.

———

"I'M STARTING A PRACTICE WITH A FRIEND," ONE OF MY classmates says. Presley? Paisley? It's one of those names. "My father is paying for the initial cost. You know…"

I tune out how her professional and personal career will be more gratifying than mine. I'd like to title this moment as, *How to Tell Your Life Sucks*.

"Well, I'm still nervous about my future," says another guy. "My employer promised a raise, but what if he fires me instead?"

"We're in high demand," another person says. "Everyone needs a physical therapist, a speech therapist, or a special ed teacher. My sister, who studied psychology, applied for a graduate degree that allows her to work as an applied behavioral therapist."

Everyone is congratulating each other about their careers and the stacks of money they'll be making once they graduate. No one's thinking about their patients.

This is depressing. Why'd I agree to have lunch with these leeches? I'm not a hermit, but let's be honest, I don't exactly mingle with my cohorts. My schedule is tight. Either I'm at school or working with one of my patients.

My options are to leave my current job and search for a practice that would pay me double or keep giving services to people who depend on the government to provide therapists. I'll stick to the latter as long as my savings can justify my morals.

My older sister says I'm an idealist, that I should be a lot more practical. I'm twenty-six and still as lost as I was when I started college.

But what's the alternative?

Am I supposed to be hopping on the capitalistic wheel where everyone is just rushing through some unfulfilled career that pays decent but sucks the life out of them?

In an ideal world, things would be different. I can't save everyone and can't do much on my own with the salary I make or could even potentially make. Which is why I do my best by working for low-income people who can't afford to send their children to therapy.

It's obvious that my income won't be high, but I'll survive.

Hopefully?

5

Eileen

AT THE END of the day, I'm emotionally and physically exhausted. Instead of going home, I go to the bar to meet one of my favorite people.

"Three weeks before the big day!" My best friend, Camilla, shouts when I squeeze into our regular booth at Finley's Pub.

"Shh," I tell her. "You're gonna jinx it."

She rolls her eyes. "Stop being paranoid."

The bar is crowded with older guys watching some sports and twenty-somethings laughing over pitchers of watered-down beer. This is our favorite bar in town because my dad used to own it, and also because it's renowned for their loaded fries and cheap beer—not because the drinks are good.

They'll go down fine enough and get me to relax to get through the week. As Camilla pours me a glass of whatever IPA we're trying tonight, I know that's all that really matters at this point in the day, week, and year.

"You know I'm right. You've seen the shit I've been through during my birthdays," I say.

"It's not that bad," she insists.

But I swear she's trying to hide a smirk.

Of course, I don't leave it at that. Instead, I bring a few nuggets from memory lane.

"Remember when Grandma Lori came to visit on my fifth birthday, and she ended up hospitalized after that bee sting," I begin. "Or remember my seventh birthday party? Joe O'Riley was playing pin the tail on the donkey, and he landed on my fucking cake."

She waves her hands and can't stop laughing at the disaster that is my birthday. I glare at her, unamused. "I'm glad you can laugh at my misfortune."

"Sorry, but you gotta admit it's a little funny."

Hilarious, I think bitterly.

At least none of them made it to *America's Funniest Home Videos.*

I grab my beer, take a sip and say, "Yeah, tragically funny. Maybe as an encore, my brother can get arrested during my graduation ceremony, or *they* can finally cancel my trip."

My parents promised this year would be different.

They even "insisted" on taking me on vacation after graduation to celebrate my birthday and that I graduated. If telling me they're finally rescheduling my birthday vacation, then telling me that I have to pay for my own way counts as a "trip."

"You'll have fun and you know it," Camilla chides me softly. "You're always saying you miss your family."

True. As much as they drive me crazy, I feel like I don't see them enough anymore. Even though they live less than twenty minutes away. We're all just too busy trying to get by.

I take another sip of my drink, taking a deep breath and letting Billy Joel's piano playing take me away for a moment.

"I guess," I concede. "As long as they don't make a scene during graduation, I'm fine. Even if they bail on me."

Speaking of which, I dig into my oversized purse for her graduation ticket. Camilla calls it my "mom friend bag." She doesn't like admitting that it's come in handy for her more than once.

"As promised," I say as I try to hand it over. "You get to celebrate my birthday and my third graduation. I'm officially out of school."

"Three degrees later, Doctor," she says and smiles sheepishly, averting her eyes.

Uh oh.

"What?" I ask as my back tenses.

She shakes her head. "I think I might be your birthday let down, babe."

"Why?" I deflate.

When push comes to shove, Camilla is always there for me. Especially when no one else will be. She's the person who bails me out when I'm in trouble. The only one who cares when I need a pint of ice cream, a stack of romantic comedies and tissues because I went through a bad breakup—or whenever my parents forget me.

Camilla takes a long chug of beer, avoiding my gaze. Great, my birthday is already disappointing and nerve-wracking.

"Work," she says. "If I could avoid it, I would. You know I hate to sleep in hotels. Let alone being away from home for six weeks." She shivers.

Camilla is the definition of a germaphobe. There was a stint in college where she'd only let me touch her stuff after using pre-sanitized hand sanitizer.

Not to mention my bag is the only other place besides her own where she can stand to keep her silverware and straw. Because that's how much Camilla hates using other people's stuff.

"When are you leaving?" I ask.

"Tomorrow, but it's okay," she says, gently patting my hand. "You're going to be away for two weeks with your family."

I stare at my glass, scratching it lightly with my thumb as if there were a label. Being with my parents isn't really something worth getting excited about. They'll be too busy checking Charlie's Instagram to make sure she's doing alright without them.

Their poor thirty-year-old daughter apparently can't survive without her parents. Or what if Sam has to stay because of some godforsaken reason? They still treat him like he is five. Who knows what the twenty-two-year-old "kid" can get into when he is unsupervised?

My trip sounds more and more like *such* a blast the closer it gets. I should've organized something with my best friend and forgotten about this ridiculous expedition my parents have been promising since I was thirteen.

Then I look at her and remember she won't be here. This year is doomed. What happened to the whole golden birthday? I'm turning twenty-seven, on the twenty-seventh of the month. That's lucky right?

I hear a snort inside my head. Clearly not.

"It'll be fine," she reassures me. "You're the most positive person I know, but when it comes to your family..."

"I'm a neurotic asshole," I concede.

"Sometimes for good reason. But what's the worst that could happen?" she asks, sounding kinda annoyed.

"I could lose my passport. Or my brother could get lost at the airport when—"

"That's the plot to Home Alone, and it's impossible to lose a twenty-two-year-old man."

"We're talking about Sam," I remind her.

"Point taken," she says. "Buy one of those child harnesses and attach it to him."

I can't help but laugh at the picture of my brother walking on a leash. He would put up a fight first and then think it's funny and act like a dog.

Fuck, someone save me. I don't think I'll survive two weeks with my parents and Sam.

———

WHEN I GET HOME, MY CAT, MAX, IS WAITING FOR ME AT the door

"Hey boy," I greet him.

"Meow," he answers, purring and rubbing his head against my leg.

"Did you miss me?" I ask as I pick him up.

"Meow!" he complains and wriggles out of my arms.

"I'll do the same with you when you climb on my bed tonight," I complain back at him. "Or when you need food."

I text my mom a quick goodnight since I forgot to finish our conversation earlier in the day.

Mom: *What are you doing up so late?*

"I'm almost twenty-seven," I complain out loud.

Max follows me around as I change. When I climb into bed, I set my phone on do not disturb mode. But not before I receive a message from my older sister.

Charlie: *Can you help me this weekend?*

I groan. She either needs a ride somewhere or she wants to borrow my car.

"Buy a car, Charlie," I mutter.

Eileen: *With?*

Charlie: *Dad might finally agree to cosign the loan for a new car.*

I stare at the phone unsure of how to answer her message. Option one, "hurray, you're finally buying a car." Option two, "what the fuck do you need me for?" Option three is, "do you even have enough money to make monthly payments?"

Charlie: *Unless you want to sign for me. I wish you were a little more supportive.*

Eileen: *I can't sign for you, Charlie.*

Charlie: *You can be a little selfish, but I forgive you.*

I spend no less than two minutes screaming into my pillow. I leave Charlie and Mom unread as I fall into a fitful sleep. Yep, my life is just peachy.

6

Jason

I'M TRYING to unwind with my favorite pastime, kicking back with a beer, crossword puzzle, and binge-watching Game of Thrones. *Trying* being the operative word because my neighbor's dog won't shut up.

The groceries that were supposed to arrive early in the morning were dropped at six. And then some delivery guy comes twenty minutes later with the wrong address. So by the third time my doorbell rings, I'm well past annoyed.

I sigh, setting my beer on my new coffee table. Maybe it's Em again, back for more pestering. Emmeline and Jack let themselves in earlier today. The not so sweet woman came by with a few new furniture pieces for my apartment.

Isn't she nice?

She used me as a fucking excuse to go antique shopping with my brother last weekend. The poor bastard is whipped to the max.

Who spends his weekends buying used shit and then refurbishes them by hand? Only an idiot in love. Who needs that kind of lame hobby?

I check the small monitor next to the door and groan. This day just keeps getting better. It's my cousin, Marek. Why today?

Why any fucking day with this clown?

"Cuz, open the door," he says showing me a six-pack.

"Go away," I shout. "The answer is no."

"Nothing says welcome to *mi casa* like 'go away,'" he says, cheerfully. "My life is a shitshow, and you don't see me yelling at you."

His life is always a shitshow.

Marek is my only cousin from my mother's side. His dad was a deadbeat and his mom—may she rest in peace—depended on my parents' help ever since. He's almost thirty and still thinks that we're his clean-up crew.

I love him like a brother, but sponsoring his art is fucking expensive.

"Hard life?" I snort as I throw the door open like a chump.

His face is as pitiful as the beer he brought me. Reluctantly, I let him in, handing him a *real* beer when we get to the kitchen. I let him grab a seat and take a sip before he ruins my night.

"What is it this time?" I ask slowly.

Marek laughs nervously. "Can't a guy come to visit his best buddy?"

Sure, if you had a "best buddy," I think.

Marek is a world-class disaster. I'm just the schmuck dumb enough to bail him out every single fucking time.

"Real subtle with the flattery, there," I say, leaving the kitchen.

"This is the last favor I ask for the rest of my life," he says finishing his beer, grabbing a new one, and following after me.

"Uh huh," I say incredulously.

He stands in the middle of my living room, squirming a bit. I honestly don't give two shits about what crisis I have to fix this time. There's a time when a guy has to say enough is enough. I just want to finish my damn show before bed.

I settle back into the couch and do just that, letting Marek flounder on his own for a bit. Then, since I really want to get back to my show, I ask, "What's the deal?"

"It's Charlie," he says finally.

"Remind me who Charlie is," I say dispassionately as I stare at the TV.

"The girl I'm dating," he explains. "You met her a couple of months ago. Jack had some office party."

I shrug because I have no idea who this Charlie person is. Marek combs through his hair with his fingers and starts pacing around the living room. He reminds me of a deer that's too skittish to be on the side of the road but too dumb to move out of the way in a safe direction.

Now that I think about it, he's been weird since he got here.

"Marek?"

"She's pregnant," he says, swallowing hard. "She's keeping it."

The fucker's practically shaking. It's weird. He's normally more laid back than I am.

"What are you going to do?" I ask.

"Is that even a question?" he says. "I'm not *him*, Jason. I'm not—I can't be my father."

I nod stiffly. "Okay, so now what?"

He takes a swig of his beer. I wince. That shit has to be lukewarm by now.

"You have to help me," he says, but it comes out sounding slightly like a demand. "I don't have a penny to my name."

"Uh, no offense, *bud*, but... what the fuck?" I utter.

What is he asking here?

He shakes his head. "This isn't another get rich quick scheme, Jay. It's about my kid."

Marek stops in front of me and says, "*Your* nice or nephew."

I scrub my face. I can feel a stress headache like no other coming on. "Why don't you ask Jack for help?"

"I was hoping you'll convince him to give me a hand too. Maybe give Charlie or me a job."

"What about your art?" I question.

Shit, I have invested years in his work. He can't just toss it away because of this. Can he? What's even the responsible call here?

"I'll stop for a couple of years until we're settled," he says.

I nod.

Who's to say he's wrong?

Then again, who's to say he has any marketable skills and can survive as a real fucking adult.

"Where are you going to live?" I ask.

He shrugs. "Charlie lives with her parents, and my studio is too small for the two of us."

I sigh, bracing myself for more bad news. "I hate to even ask, but...how old is this Charlie?"

"Twenty-nine," he says. "She's between jobs."

Of course she's between jobs and dating Marek. He looks like a million bucks, but his bank account is drier than the Sahara Desert.

"Look, if you help me fix this, I'll never ask for anything ever again," he pleads.

I snicker. He won't ask me for anything, until the next time he fucks up.

But I guess that makes us both fools. He believes this is the last one—and so do I.

————

"CALL THE FOUR SEASONS OR THE RITZ-CARLTON HOTEL," JACK says as I keep browsing my phone for a wedding helper or whatever.

Twelve hours and six cups of coffee later, Jack and I are on one of his ugly ass couches pulling together a shotgun wedding.

"What's the name of those organizing wedding people?" I ask Emmeline.

"You mean a wedding planner?" She smirks amused.

"I guess. You know any?" I ask, playing dumb and waiting for her to take over for us.

Weddings aren't my scene. In fact, I hate weddings and the whole concept of marriage. It's just a dumb way to attach yourself to another person who will let you down one way or another.

She grins and I divert my gaze.

"You do have a heart, don't you?" She asks, and I can hear the satisfaction in her voice.

I keep my eyes plastered to my phone. "I have no idea what you're talking about."

"Uh huh," she says. "What happened to let's stop fixing Marek's life? You're both a couple of gullible saps for trying to pull together a last-minute wedding and making it good."

"We can't leave him high and dry. We're all he has," I argue meeting her gaze.

"Don't you think the bride should get some input in all this?" She arches her eyebrow.

"Marek says she's just as lost as he is," Jack finally speaks.

Sometimes I feel like he enjoys when his lovely woman makes me squirm. Fucker.

She shakes her head and rolls her eyes. "Even if that's the case, you can give them a hand. Not just do everything for them. Suggest the venues, but let them choose. I bet she has a favorite color. What if you choose bubble gum pink and she hates it?"

"Personally, I'm more of a black and teal guy," I joke.

"Call him, ask him to bring his girlfriend. Or maybe you can get the families together," she suggests ignoring my joke.

That idea isn't too bad, until I remember one little detail, "Our parents are in Athens."

"You two will be there," she says. "Maybe Jeannette can join. I know June is working on a project so don't count on her. Alex's week should be clear. His physical therapist is on vacation."

I grimace at Jack. "Does she have our schedules memorized?"

Jack smiles and shakes his head. "She talks or chats with our sisters daily and with Alex even more. Aren't you coming too, Em? I'm counting on your contacts to get some of this done."

She winks at him and says, "To the family reunion? No. I'll give you my contacts, but it's going to cost you."

"It's a price I'm willing to pay," he answers. "Some sacrifices will be made, but I'll submit to any of your wishes to make up for your services."

"I wouldn't expect any less from you," she pauses, licking her lips. "Mr. Spearman."

"Incredible. My powers of invisibility have grown. Next stop, NORAD. I'm stealing one of their fancy airplanes," I say deadpan.

They kiss and ignore me.

My body freezes for a moment.

I hate being the petty third wheel, but what else is there for me?

Somedays, their love is just too much and too depressing. It threatens to push me toward the past and drown me with the memories of what I once dreamed and can never have. Not that I want some shitty relationship. There's no fucking way I'll gamble on love again.

I glance at them and repeat inside my head, *never again.*

7

Eileen

THE INEVITABLE SENSATION of nostalgia mixed with despair churns in my stomach as I approach my parents' house. I love my family, but sometimes I feel like an outsider. Scratch that, I always feel like an outsider.

I am the afterthought.

My sister is the eldest and everything that happens to her is a novelty. My youngest brother is the baby, and who knows why, but he's always in trouble. I can fend for myself, according to my family. So, there's nothing left of my parents' minimal attention worth sparing on me.

I don't expect a lot from my family. A lot of the time I expect nothing because that's just easier. It's been proven time and time again that I'm their last priority, if even at all.

When I park in front of my childhood home and spot not one, but three more cars than usual, I know they aren't going to care about my graduation tickets. Something a lot more important is brewing at the McBean residence.

Who cares? I tell myself.

Logically speaking, it can't be any worse than the thousands of other "emergencies" that have usurped me over the years.

I hear the commotion as I enter the house. Everyone is talking and of course no one's making any fucking sense. My sister screams hysterically.

Typical Charlie, I think.

The guy who she's been dating for the last couple of months is right next to her staring into the wall and looking pale. Okay that, admittedly, is weird.

Who died?

Mom is on her phone. Dad is pacing back and forth. My grandmother is taking a page out of my sister's book, squawking and screaming. My grandfather is sitting in the corner of the couch watching TV like nothing's happening. Maybe he got lucky and went deaf in the middle of this hell storm. My brother is on the other side of the couch, staring at his phone.

At least some things never change around here.

I'm pleasantly surprised my aunts and uncles aren't part of this chaos. I look at the white envelope I hold with my graduation tickets. I sigh, putting them back in my purse. Maybe some other time.

I should leave before they see me and drag me into whatever's happening. It's only a few steps, I almost make it to the door when someone taps my shoulder. It's Sam.

"Forget it. I'm not saving you from whatever shit is happening," I say, grabbing the door handle.

"The 'artist' knocked *her* up," he says.

"You're making shit up," I counteract his statement. "She won't be happy when she hears that."

"Nope," he says deadpan.

I let go of the handle, groaning as I rub my temple. "Please, please, please tell me this is a fucking fever dream, or I'm on *Punk'd* or something."

"I wish," he grunts. "Charlie's pregnant. Sound the alarms, the world's ending. Mom and Dad are already moving her into an emergency bunker."

I chuckle because he's not wrong about how our parents overreact whenever Charlie's involved. This really sounds like something that's going to take about eighteen to twenty years to get resolved. And make no mistake. I want no part in it.

"Well, Tiger," I call him with the nickname Dad used for him when he was younger. "Good luck with this shit. Hope you find a job before *Charlie* turns your room into a nursery."

"Ha ha. Hilarious," he says.

Obviously, he's not in the mood for sarcasm, and I can't believe he made it this far in the day without picking up and leaving. I'm ready to change my name, get a new face, and move to Canada, and I've known for all of three minutes.

But who could blame me?

One way or another, my parents are going to make me part of the solution. I salute him before opening the door. *See you in a couple of decades... or never.*

But before I can turn around and leave, Charlie charges at me.

"E!" She doesn't even bother to call me by my full name. "You're here."

Fantastic. I look at the ceiling hoping for a miracle and nothing. The ground isn't swallowing me either.

I'm doomed.

Charlie hugs me tightly while she continues sobbing. "You have to help me. Please. I don't know what to do!"

Of course you don't, I think tersely. That's just who you are, Charlie.

———

FEELING SOMEWHAT DAZED AFTER DEALING WITH MY FAMILY, I decide to stay at my parents to help my sister. I'm sitting alone in their living room with nothing but a lamp, a pen, and my journal to keep me company.

I've been tapping my pen against my journal for the last hour, hoping it calms my nerves, annoys me out of my funk, rallies me into action... something. The rhythm keeps me company in the loneliest corner of the Earth, shielding me from the fucking bullshit that's become my life.

I shouldn't enable her, but that's like the family motto. "Charlie first."

Charlie left early with her loser boyfriend because she's "tired." Mom went to bed because she has to go to work tomorrow morning. Which leaves me, once again behind picking up the debris of the mayhem my sister and the rest of my family left behind.

Because of course, it's Eileen's responsibility to create a plan of action.

I don't envy my sister. Sure, she drives me fucking bonkers. But she's a grown woman who can't even take care of herself. If anything, I feel sorry that my years of enabling have left her so sorely unprepared to have a baby.

Then again, she loves pretending to be fragile so everyone would do anything for her. I swear she just bats her eyelashes and everyone is at her feet asking what she needs. Maybe I should ignore her pleas, but if I do, my parents would be stuck doing everything for her.

In conclusion, me sitting alone in my parents' house to plan a fucking wedding for my pregnant sister is *of course*, my own fault. Surfing through bridal websites, checking dresses and destination weddings isn't something I really want to do. The cost of a wedding is outrageous.

Where are we going to find the money to afford any of this?

I look at my calendar and sigh. I thought my parents were going to cancel the trip. Logically, I knew that we'd have to cancel it. Since I insisted on buying the vacation insurance, we should have been able to recover almost everything minus the two hundred and sixty dollars of insurance. "Should have" being the operative term.

They waited until Charlie left—until I suggested we cancel the trip—to admit they hadn't booked anything on their end.

"It was a big financial commitment. We were waiting on a few things before we finalized plans," my mom told me.

Waiting on what?

Me to flunk grad school?

For me to break another bone... or worse?

There's no money to recover because they'd never spent a dime on the vacation they promised me. So, if I understand everything right, the *budget* for the trip is going into Charlie's wedding fund.

Camilla called me crazy. A neurotic loon. Well, here I am proving her wrong and unable to call her because she's off of the grid.

But I knew that everything was too good to be true.

Once I have a list of websites, possible places to have the ceremony, and bridal stores, I decide it's okay to go to bed.

Charlie insists we should hire Amanda, her best friend from high school, to plan the wedding. I don't want to hire a wedding planner. My parents haven't given me a final budget yet, but I know it's not going to be enough to pay Amanda's rates.

So long, Aruba, I think mournfully.

It was fun dreaming of you while it lasted. As I start making my way to my old room, the home phone rings. Seriously, who calls at almost two a.m.? It better not be Charlie complaining about heartburn. I have no more patience for her today.

"Hello," I answer curtly.

"Is this the McBean residence?" a sexy, husky voice asks on the other side.

"Yes..." I confirm, staring at the phone for a second. Who is this? "Can I help you?"

"Uh, I'm looking for Marek."

Who the fuck is Marek?

"You have the wrong number," I say before hanging up.

Nice voice. His call doesn't make any sense to me, but I wouldn't mind him selling me shit over the phone if I get to hear his baritone.

The phone rings again. "Didn't you *just* say that this is the McBean residence?" he argues the moment I answer.

"Yeah, but no one named *Marek* lives here," I counteract.

"You have the wrong number," I clarify, pausing between words so he can understand me.

"Look, lady, I'm looking for my cousin, Marek. He's supposed to be with Charlie," he explains with a condescending voice. "You know Charlie, right?"

I roll my eyes. Don't try me buddy, I don't have much patience left.

"Oh, that guy," I say. "The *artist* Charlie's dating."

He chuckles and asks, "Is he there?"

"No," I answer a little short. Why is he looking for his cousin here? "Don't you have his cell number?"

"Duh," he says. "But he's not answering, and we need to talk."

"Why would you call here then?"

"This is Charlie's number, isn't it?" he asks.

Yes, because my sister can't afford to live on her own, but she can drop four hundred and fifty dollars on the Tori Burch purse she drags everywhere. Priorities, I guess.

"Nope, they're not here. Don't know where they went, and I don't know when they'll be back," I half lie.

"He's not answering his cell," he says again with a resigned sigh. "Well, fuck it. This is the last time I try to save his ass."

Well at least someone else is as annoyed with them as I am. Maybe I'm not alone in wading through their pre-marital chaos.

"Let me guess," I infer, taking the phone with me to my room. "He needs you to bail him out of his latest problem?"

"Yep," he says with a yawn. "News travels fast or—"

"I think I can relate," I admit. "I just spent the last two hours doing recon for this wedding they just *have to have*."

"Why you and not Charlie?"

I snort. "She's allergic to responsibility. Or even, like, committing to plans beyond vague ideas."

"Ouch," he says with a chuckle. "That bad, huh?"

I glance over at a family portrait from a decade ago. Charlie's crying in the center between my parents because of a bee sting, Sam's screaming, and I'm tripping into the frame because of a mud patch no one bothered to mention.

My parents framed it because they said they wanted a reminder of who we were growing up. I'm starting to think we'll never get past that awkward phase of life. So maybe things are meant to suck.

"Isn't it always?" I say to him, myself, and no one in particular.

"Not sure," he says genuinely. "People keep telling me there's better shit out there but—"

"Where?" we say simultaneously.

I snort. "Jesus fuck, we sound tired."

"Well it is ass o'clock."

"I meant about life," I explain further.

"I know," he states, his voice a tad defeated. I've never seen this guy, but I imagine he pauses to shrug before he says, "But hey, you sound not terrible."

"Thanks?" I respond to his statement, unsure if I should be offended.

"You ever planned a wedding?" he asks.

"No, but, I'm a fast learner."

"Cool." He sounds animated. "What's your rate? Some charge two hundred an hour."

What? "I'm not a hooker," I squeak.

"I meant wedding planner," he corrects, but he's laughing his ass off on the other side of the line.

"Who are you?"

"Oh, shit, sorry," he says, sobering up. "Jason, cousin of the idiot groom. And you are?"

"Eileen, sister of the idiot bride."

"Nice to meet a future in-law," he jokes. "Marek convince me to give him a hand with his situation."

I nod slowly and then realize he can't see me. "Cool, you'll be the company to my misery then, and you don't sound terrible either."

He sighs. "Fair enough. I hope to meet you soon," he says with a low, sexy voice that makes my body tingle.

"Same," I whisper before hanging up.

8

Jason

MAREK'S FIANCÉE IS, in a word, yikes.

Don't get me wrong, she's hot. Medium height, skinny enough, nice rack, good ass, and kinda blonde just like her eyes are kinda green. Too bad you can't see most of that over the sound of her screaming every fucking hour of the day.

And what does she even do for a living? I tuned her out after she started saying "semi-professional amateur street activism slash entre-preneurialism."

So, in short, good body, horrible personality. On the bright side, I've never seen someone give an impassioned ten-minute speech about how shitty their soda is before.

"Just two cubes. If you add too many, it's too cold and my throat hurts." She clears her throat, pouting her lips and lowering her gaze.

I try to catch Marek's gaze. I just want a confirmation that this woman is for real and not an actor on some shitty *Punk'd* reboot. But judging by the way he kisses her temple, maybe he's just fucked.

The saying is true though, you don't choose who you fall in love with. R.I.P. Marek's sanity.

I'd give it a year. Maybe he'll learn his lesson and just pay child support. Or maybe they'll figure out they don't live in the fucking 1950s and they don't have to get married to raise a kid.

Who am I kidding? The poor spawn is fucked either way.

"We'll need a house," she says apropos of nothing. "Your studio is too tiny, and you need a place for your art."

"He can't afford a house," I inform her, in case she hasn't realized that my cousin is broke.

Woman, get a clue!

She makes some sort of whining sound, like a wounded animal. "I thought his family would be helping him."

Listen, there's a huge difference between helping and supporting his lifestyle for the rest of his natural life. I open my mouth to give her a lecture, but what's the point?

"Who said anything about paying for a house?" I glare at Marek.

Seriously, dude, what the fuck did you tell her? I think, but I save it for when we are alone.

"Mar, you said we'd buy a new house for our baby," she squeaks. "We have to give her the very best, remember?"

She's either the dumbest person or the smartest con artist I've ever met. Regardless, this is hell. How do we even know she's pregnant? Or that the baby is Marek's?

"Yeah, I'm not buying anyone a house," I announce.

"No worries, dude. I have a few job interviews lined up," Marek informs with his chill voice. "We just need the initial push."

That's a relief to me, but Charlie gets a really weird, tight smile, so tight that I'm afraid she might pummel me.

"I won't be moving to an apartment," Charlie says firmly. "If it all comes to the worst, we can use Eileen's bedroom for the baby. She doesn't need it anymore. You can use Sam's bedroom as your shop, or we can convince Dad to keep the cars outside and convert the garage into your studio."

I run a hand through my hair. Marek's studio apartment is *quaint* at best. At least the peeling wooden panel walls look intentional, or "stylish." On second thought, there's probably some health hazards around here considering how "thoughtful" these jokers are.

"What is it that you do again?" I ask her.

"I'm an assistant manager at Neiman Marcus," she says flattening her clothes. "But I don't think I'll be able to continue working there."

"She could work for Em," I suggest. "Be a virtual assistant."

Marek smiles and says, "That's a great idea."

Of course Charlie fucking pouts. "I thought we agreed I wouldn't work for the first few years, Mar. Someone has to look after the baby."

Gotta say, she's fucking persistent. I sigh, kicking back the rest of the water Marek offered me like it's beer. Where is the alcohol? Actually, I gotta get out of here before I open my big mouth.

"Well, this has been fun," I tell Marek with a pat on the back. "Maybe start with something small like budgeting or childproofing this place a little. I'll see what I can find in terms of cheap home rentals, but I'm not doing any heavy lifting for you."

Charlie goes beet red. Great, she has even more emotions. What now?

"Do you think we're not responsible enough to take care of our own kid?" she questions angrily.

I choose to ignore her tone as I head out the front door. "Glad we're on the same page. I'll make sure Emmeline gets in touch with you. The sooner you switch jobs, the better."

"Cuz," Marek calls out as I reach the door. "Don't forget we're having dinner at her parents' on Sunday. They want to meet the fam."

Fuck, these two are wearing down my patience and asking for way too much of me. "Sure, just send me the address."

———

I GREW UP IN A LOUD, CLOSE-KNIT, CRAZY FAMILY. THERE'S NO

other way to describe the Spearman clan. Three boys, twin girls, and lots of cousins from the Spearman side. Family reunions are fun and yet chaos.

Being the middle child has its benefits, mostly. It means I've seen my fair share of stupendously loud arguments and ruckus events. It also means that when Jack, fairly, escapes from bullshit situations, I'm next in line to be "the responsible one."

I never thought there'd be a family louder than mine. Cue the McBeans, proving me wrong with every passing second. There are about twenty conversations going on at once, so I gave up early on trying to understand anything going on around me.

If I have to guess, there are easily five generations of family crammed into this four-bedroom home. I keep getting knocked into by my future in-laws, asking me "which one" am I and "why's your plate so empty?" I'm half convinced these people are trying to fatten me up to serve me as the main course.

Around eight, people start filtering out. I take that as my cue to finally duck out, so I look for Marek to say goodbye.

"Wait, we have to talk about the wedding and the b-a-b-y," he says. Because nothing is ever one and done with him.

"Why are you spelling that?"

"Some of them don't know about it yet," he says.

I roll my eyes. Some days I'm amazed that he can get out of bed by himself. "Dude, they know how to spell."

He shrugs. "Still, I need you to stay, please."

I nod in resignation, getting comfortable on the couch again. What's another hour dealing with this crowd? Seriously, what's the worst that can happen? At least it's gotten quieter around here.

"No, Mom," Charlie shrieks. "Why would I want fuchsia as a color for my wedding?"

"She's at it already. Impressive," a woman says behind me.

When I look over my shoulder, I spot a short, curvy chick standing by the entryway. She stares at Charlie. She's cute, her dark, curly hair tucked underneath a green beanie that matches her eyes and jacket. She glances at me, giving me a once over. She scrunches her nose.

Why haven't I seen her before? Huh, maybe she's a new guest.

I wave at her awkwardly and walk toward her. She quirks her lips. Pretty sure she's laughing at me under her breath. It's fine, I probably have a stupid look on my face.

"Come here often?" I ask. "Seems like you're a pro."

"Hardly," she says while taking her things off. "I'm just the unfortunate spawn they had after that one."

"I take it you're the understudy?" I ask as we sit down on the couch.

She laughs. "God no. More like the shortstop."

I chuckle. She feels so familiar, like a song I forgot I love. Then I remember my conversation over the phone a few nights ago. "Eileen, right?"

"Yep, and you must be Jason," she states dryly. "Nice to meet you... again."

"Ditto," I say, and then, as I glance over to a half-full house, point out, "You missed the family reunion."

"That was intentional," she confesses. "The key is to always have an excuse. Show up late and with a full stomach. It's the only way to survive around here."

Wish I had known that five hours ago. "Noted," I say, patting my stomach.

"Do they know about the baby?" she mumbles.

I raise my eyebrow confused. "Your parents?"

"No, the rest of the family." She looks around as if taking inventory of the place. "I guess not, or they'd still be hovering around *her*."

She wasn't kidding on the phone when she said it's always rough. I've known the McBeans for a few hours, and I'm tapped out.

But an entire lifetime?

Eileen's a trooper, and a funny one to boot.

"So, what's next?" I ask curiously.

She shushes me and redirects my head toward where her mother is pacing in the kitchen.

"It has to happen fast, Murphy," her mom says to her dad. "You don't want her to show. Everyone will know."

"The horror," Eileen whispers, clutching her jacket.

I swallow a laugh.

"I wish I had brought popcorn to watch this," she says, crossing her arms. "Next, my sister will fake like she's offended. Then Mom will say something to upset her even more."

"We don't have money for a big party, Lorena," Mr. McBean clarifies.

"There are always ways," Mrs. McBean insists.

This is like a tennis match. I don't know who is keeping score, but my bet is on Mrs. McBean. My father has one rule, never contradict your mother. Also, he always lets her win. I guess those are *two* big rules.

"How do you think we raised three children? Charlie will use my dress."

"Oh no, 'used' dress. That's strike two," Eileen mumbles.

She was right about one thing. We need popcorn.

"What do you mean?" Charlie shrieks. "You're shorter than me, and I can't be wearing your dress. It's for your wedding. I need something for me. Why can't you be a little nice to me!? Don't you see I'm hurting?"

"She's a great actress," I say for the first time out loud. "Didn't buy it at first but hey, what a performance."

"One of the best, such a pity she didn't go to Hollywood." Then, Eileen exhales. "You should leave before this becomes a circus."

I look around waiting for the clowns and the lion tamer. "Why?"

"She's about to search for her next target or someone to fix her life. I bet it'll be me. Mom will do the same, and by the end of the night, everything for this fucking wedding will officially be my responsibility."

"Do you have money for it?" I ask.

"I'm a physical therapist who works for the government," she answers. "You tell me."

"We're going to have to bail them out," I conclude.

"Nope, not tonight," she clarifies.

"Wanna get out of here before they catch you?" I offer. "We can ask them to brunch tomorrow. Talk shit out with fewer people."

She looks like I just told her she won the lottery, nodding as she grabs her jacket and pulls me quietly toward the door. We don't say anything until we're inside the front seats of a beat-up Subaru, backing out of the driveway.

It smells like lavender and regret (or maybe just really old vomit stains). She puts on some Eddie Money track and laughs like an escaped convict. I feel laughter bubbling up in me and realize fuck, I must feel it too.

It's the first time since Marek dropped this fucking baby bomb on me that I've felt like I had any choice in the matter.

"We made it," she says excitedly. "Mom's going to freak later about me skipping dinner."

"What're you gonna tell her?"

"Work," she says with a shrug. "I have to write down a plan for the people who'll be taking over for me while I'm on vacation."

"Nice," I offer conversationally. "Where are you going?"

She cocks an eyebrow. "You're kidding, right? Didn't you see that madness? I need time off to deal with it."

I nod, letting her drive us into the fucking sunset.

"So, now that we're co-conspirators in a getaway with no discernible place to go... Do you wanna grab a drink?"

She laughs like a songbird. "Sure."

9

Eileen

JASON IS... interesting.

On the one hand, his physique and beer choice scream trust fund frat boy.

On the other hand, he spent an hour last night at one of my favorite bars talking about the best way to arrange centerpieces with the kind of sincerity and knowledge most dudes wouldn't give to anything, let alone a cousin's wedding.

His eyes lit up when, upon leaving, he asked what my coffee order is and I said, "Preferably espresso, but anything as long as it's strong enough to wake up the dead."

I showed up to brunch this morning not expecting a flight of espressos to sample.

"Are you serious? Is this some kind of challenge?" I ask him, trying to suppress a grin.

He smirks. "It's only a challenge if you make it one."

We're buzzed by the time Charlie and Marek arrive. Charlie wrinkles her nose at the sight of coffee. I catch Jason's gaze, rolling my eyes subtly. He nearly chokes on his orange juice.

It's fascinating watching him switch from *giant goof* to *serious businessman* once Charlie and Marek get settled. As he goes over the job he's helping Marek get, I study his profile.

Masculine nose, sensual mouth, strong, chiseled jaw with a pair of high cheekbones framing those warm brown eyes that keep staring at me when he thinks nobody is watching.

"I have a job," Charlie snaps when he turns his attention to her.

Of course, she just got hired at Neiman Marcus three weeks ago. How long until she quits?

"You said it yourself. Once the baby arrives you can't do retail," I remind her. "Consider your options, Charlie."

"Easy for you to say. If you were pregnant, you'd be fine," she says, adding a pout. "You have a job that will give you maternity leave and benefits."

Sure, let's talk about how my low-income job is suddenly much better than any other job in the whole fucking world. Poor little Charlie, she has it rough.

"What happened to your benefits?" I ask instead.

"They'll be gone once I quit," she says.

Make up your mind, Charlie. Do you have a job or not?

I take a deep breath and then say, "Then don't quit. Or get hired by someplace that has more competitive benefits. Doesn't Marek have insurance?"

Jason gives me a look that feels like "we're screwed, aren't we?"

Okay, let's handle this another way.

I grab a pen and my journal out of my purse. "Let's start with what we absolutely have to get done today. Housing, jobs, and preliminary wedding details. Alright?"

"Please, you have to help me with the last one," Charlie whines. "Did I tell you Mom wants me to wear her dress?"

Well, I guess we're shifting priorities. Why not? It's not like having a roof over your head and a way to support your kid matters.

"What's their budget for the wedding?" I ask.

I've been dodging Mom's calls for the past couple of days. There's not a snowball's chance in hell I'll call her to ask that. There's too high a risk of hearing *everything* about yesterday's reunion-slash-meeting.

"They said it's small," she says with a soft voice.

Typical Charlie, she's about to give me a sob story to convince me that I have to do something to make her dreams come true.

"You know what that means, right?" She sighs. "Ceremony in the backyard, honeymoon in Idaho Springs, and if I'm lucky, she'll make some corned beef casserole surprise and seven-layer-bean-cheese dip."

I glare at her. Sometimes she makes us sound like a cheap version of some crazy sitcom. Yes, Mom tends to be frugal. But she does it mostly with family who doesn't care.

If there's a wedding where she has to show everyone that she's Lorena McBean, then it'll be a high-end event.

Which we can't afford!

Either way, we're screwed.

"Look, I canceled the trip and got a full refund," I lie. "Why don't we plan the wedding with it?"

"That was less than ten thousand dollars, Eileen. The dress I want costs twenty thousand."

"We'll find a cheaper dress, a better one," I suggest, sounding convincing.

I make a mental note to check online for used dresses or maybe an outlet. Do they even exist?

"Honey," I say, reaching for her hand to squeeze it. "As much as I'd love for you to have a wedding as close as possible to what Meghan Markle had, we can't. Our resources are limited."

"I can help with some of the expenses," Jason offers.

Seriously, you have no idea what you're getting into, buddy, I think. But I only glare at him.

"Within reason," he corrects.

My sister's smile brightens, and she pulls out her phone. "Make sure you choose everything based on what's on our wedding Pinterest board, Eileen."

"What?" I ask. I expected to have to plan the wedding but— "Why the Pinterest board?"

"You've said it yourself a million times," she explains. "I'm terrible at sticking to a budget. If you're going to limit me, you'll have to put in the work. Besides, everything I like is on there. It's not like you need me micromanaging you when my dream wedding is all there."

Charlie tucks a stray piece of hair behind her ear casually. As if she didn't just tell me to use "our" –really *my*—dream wedding plans to do all the dirty work for her.

"When's the wedding, anyway?" I ask numbly.

She looks at the calendar on her phone and says, "May twenty-seventh."

"What?" I say in disbelief. "You can't be serious. That's my—"

"Eileen, could you please stop thinking about yourself," Charlie shouts so loud everyone in the restaurant stops talking. A few women glare at me. "Look at me. I'm in the middle of a crisis. You can reschedule whatever you had penciled in for some other time."

Cool, let me grab my time machine, go back twenty-seven years and make sure that Mom waits a day or two to have me.

While I'm at it, I'll make sure to force my university to change graduation dates. Because Charlie always comes first. What she wants, she gets. Everything else is just a fucking afterthought.

I clear my throat. I ignore Jason's confused gaze, instead fixating on the short stack of pancakes in front of me.

"Sure, Charlie," I say quietly. "Whatever you want."

10

Eileen

Fourteen days until the wedding

MAY BRINGS sporadic snowfall to Colorado, it also brings the warmest days since December and miles and miles of sunshine. I roll the passenger seat window of Jason's luxury car all the way down, letting my hand dangle outside. My fingers dance against the breeze.

"Geez, we can put the air conditioner on," Jason mutters.

I roll my head over to stare at him incredulously. "It's not about the temperature in here, bud."

He shrugs.

"Try it," I say. "Feel the breeze."

"No offense but that sounds like hippie shit," Jason says.

"No offense but you've been here for what? A year?"

"Yeah," he concedes.

"*You* are officially hippie shit," I argue.

He grumbles halfheartedly as he rolls his own window down.

Trying not to test his patience, it feels like a good time to get back to business. As I go through the bullet points and realize how many things we have to do, I'm wondering how we're going to get everything done. The venue is, of course, the biggest ticket item by far.

Jason's driving us to Boulder, where he found a place similar to what Charlie is looking for. One of her options is essentially Niagara Falls meets the Rocky Mountains.

The second is a fucking palace and her last option, which cracks me up, an expensive hotel. That's exactly how she described it. So that's all we've got.

I texted her last night, suggesting a destination wedding.

You know, something exclusive that's luxurious but will naturally keep attendance down without hurting anyone's feelings.

She called me a minute later to give me a ten-minute lecture about how "important" it is to stick to the Pinterest board. That *if* the time ever comes, I can plan my own fucking wedding however I want.

I tuned her out after that point. There's only so much screaming I can take from her in a single sitting.

If I was the one getting married, however, I wouldn't choose a palace. I can't imagine having my first dance to John Mellencamp in a building that's older than the state I grew up in. I sigh and decide that no matter what, I will find a venue for this wedding today.

Speak of the devil, Mellencamp starts playing long enough for Jason to skip the song to Springsteen of all things.

"What the fuck?" I protest.

"What?"

I glare at the dashboard and then at him. "I can't believe you just did that—"

"Putting on good music?" he asks incredulously. "Yeah, you're welcome."

I jostle his shoulder with my elbow. "How dare you insult John Mellencamp like that?"

"What—oh," he says incredulously. "Really? A Mellencamp girl. Didn't think you existed anymore."

Apparently, it's my turn to be confused. "What?"

"Look," he says, "There are three kinds of people in the world: Springsteen people, Bon Jovi people, and Mellencamp people. Springsteen people rule. Bon Jovi people are—"

"Careful," I warn him. "My parents are *Bon Jovi* people."

"—Wrong but whatever." He shrugs.

He presses his lips together making a long pause and then continues, "Those are the two main factions. And Mellencamp people are different. Underdogs."

"Underdog?" I question his sanity.

"Hey," he says reaching out to squeeze my hand lightly. "I guess it's just about who you grew up with and what their music does for you."

I hum, mulling it all over. We speed by the mountains which somedays are the most real thing in my life.

"They played a lot of Mellencamp and Petty here, back in the day," I explain. "I guess there was Bon Jovi, whose stuff was a lot more popular. Mellencamp's music was about trying your best and stumbling through life, not always getting your way, but surviving."

"See?" he says. "Underdog through and through."

I huff. "How far away is this place?"

"Not too far," he says. "Just a few more miles."

I stare at the mountain scenery. The evergreens are still covered with some snow that fell last weekend. It's a beautiful sight but not for a wedding.

"Just not yours," Jason says.

"Did you read my mind?" I ask.

"Yeah, I wish," he says confidently before blushing. "Come on, you must have thought about your wedding, haven't you?"

Ordinarily, I don't dream about my wedding. But I'd be lying if I say that I've never thought about it.

"It's complicated," I answer. Shall we go through the obvious, the fucking Pinterest board Charlie is making me use is mainly mine.

"If I married, I'd definitely want something small," I say a little dishearten.

Because if I ever get married, I can't use any of these ideas, or I'd be copying Charlie. She'll throw a tantrum in the middle of the ceremony or refuse to let the priest continue with it until the flowers were changed.

Maybe I should be the one organizing a destination wedding. Only a few guests. No children. *Oops, sorry, Charlie. You can't join us.*

"That doesn't answer my question," he observes. "If it were me getting married in the mountains, I'd choose the Shining."

I do a double take. "What do you mean with you'd choose *The Shining?*"

"There's a hotel in Estes Park we could rent," he says enthusiastically. "You think your sister would go with for that? It'd be a good excuse to use a black dress."

I gawk at him. "You mean The Stanley Hotel?"

"The very one," he says proudly. "I already made some calls. If you want it, they'll let us rent out the whole thing for the weekend. It's expensive as fuck, but we can make it happen."

I groan. "We have a budget."

"It could be my wedding gift to them," he continues, ignoring my glare. "We can get them *the* room for the weekend. Marek would love it."

Somehow, I think he's just fucking with me.

"So what?" I play along with his little wedding fantasy. Seriously, *The Shining?* No wonder he is single. "If you get The Stanley Hotel, are you planning on handing out signed books and the DVD as party favors?"

"Oh, that's a good idea," he says, and I finally notice his wicked smile.

"You're so not funny," I say, barely concealing my own smile. "Honestly, I'd rather have a normal hotel for a wedding than these *spectacular gardens* in the *middle of the majestic woods* next to a *crystal-clear* waterfall."

"Alright, now we're getting somewhere." He says as licks his full lips. "What do we have to do to make that happen? What do you have in mind?"

"The Broadmoor would be fantastic if we could actually get it," I say, knowing full well that it's always booked.

"Done and done," he says as he taps some of the buttons on his dashboard.

"Hey," he says as he pulls over to the shoulder. "Do you think Em can get us the Broadmoor."

"You've officially gone crazy," I mutter.

"I'm dictating a text to my brother," he answers. "His girlfriend has *connections*. Maybe we can get a slot for that day to get these two hitched. You think your sister would change her mind about the day?"

I laugh. He hasn't spent enough time with Charlie, but I bet that by the end of this affair he's going to stay at least a town away from my sister and our entire family at all times.

"Like my sister would care about changing her date," I say trying to control the laugh. "She said May twenty-seventh and that would be it."

"So, there's no room to negotiate?"

"Any time would really work," I tell him. If there's something I've learned after all these years, is to work with loopholes. "Regardless, we'll have to make sure everyone who comes from out of town makes it on time."

"Your parents do a lot for her, don't they?"

I don't answer.

He puts the car in drive, peeling back onto the highway. "Okay once we have the venue, what's next?"

Checking on my journal, I say, "Charlie's working on the guest list. Thank fuck she gets that we can't invite more than a hundred people..."

"I hear a 'but', Eileen," he says with a voice akin to a sports announcer.

"Well, Jason," I say, matching his tone. "It's still anyone's guess if she'll actually *stay* under a hundred people. Let alone how many people she'll try to squeeze into her bridal party."

We're still heading in the direction of Boulder. There's a shop that does custom wedding invites that Charlie "has" to have.

Clouds roll by overhead, dwarfing us with their shadows. Jason goes back to comfortably dangling his left hand out the window. I don't say, *I told you so,* but it feels good to be right.

It isn't until we get off the highway that I realize I messed up by adding *Save the Date.* There's no fucking way we can send the cards.

I text Charlie, asking if she wants to create an event online instead.

Eileen: *Do you want to create a Save the Date online?*

Charlie: *Dang, That's a little tacky, don't you think?*

No, I think that's the only way I can get it done on time, but I don't type the response.

Charlie: *Is there any way that we can send them tonight instead?*

Before I can answer, another text pops with yet another ridiculous question.

Charlie: *When are you guys organizing the engagement party?*

My jaw drops. My stomach is churning. She's on my last nerve and this wedding is just getting started. I try to keep my anger at bay.

"She wants an engagement party," I announce, baffled, angry, and yet sounding flat.

"Seriously?" Jason says as he parks in front of the card shop.

His phone buzzes and a message appears on the screen of his dashboard.

Jack: *If you can be at the Broadmoor Hotel within the next couple of hours, they might be able to find something for you.*

Jason: *Why a couple of hours?*

Jack: *The event coordinator leaves at three.*

"It's one," I say staring at the message on his dashboard.

"Well fuck," he says. "Shit. Okay, let's go in the shop, ask for what's on your list and then leave. Ten minutes, tops."

"Cool," I say as casually as possible.

By the look on Jason's face, it isn't reassuring to either of us.

11

Jason

IT'S a *perfect* day to take one last trip to Steamboat before the season closes.

But where am I?

Racing from Boulder back to Colorado Springs to look at a wedding venue for my cousin and his high-maintenance fiancée. Marek fucking owes me. Way to ruin my weekend, buddy.

When I heard they would extend the ski season this year, I was so excited. But look how well that worked out. Saturdays are supposed to be fun days.

I don't ask for much. I just need a place, a plan, a beautiful companion, and a bottle of liquor.

See? Straight forward, nice and easy. That keeps me satiated for an entire weekend. It really doesn't take much to keep me happy and satisfied.

What's abso-fucking-lutely not satisfying, is touring the grounds of the Broadmoor to scout the perfect place for a shotgun wedding.

"So, what's wrong with Vegas again?" I suggest, half joking.

Eileen shrugs. "Nothing. It's a great town. Lots of movies take place there. I don't know why people hate on it so much."

"But for a shotgun wedding or maybe eloping?" I clarify. "My assistant can make the reservations. I'll get a plane. We'll be there before six. There are plenty of venues. We could probably pick one on the spot."

She laughs. Like seriously laughs for about a minute like I just said the funniest, most amazing joke in the history of jokes.

When she finally sobers up, she asks with that curious voice, "Did you run that idea by Charlie already?"

I rub the back of my neck sheepishly. "No."

"Well if you do," she says excitedly, and that excites me too. Finally, I found the solution to end this madness. "I want to be right there. I'll have my camera ready."

Is she mocking me?

I shoot her an unimpressed frown. "I'm not joking."

"Me neither." She shakes her head, laughing once again. "She'll try to kill you right on the spot. That's worth taping."

"Oh, come on. It's a great idea," I insist.

"You're talking about my sister," she says, waving the wedding journal in my face. "She thinks the only wedding worth having is a wedding that's as glamorous as a royal affair."

"We could make Vegas glamorous," I grumble.

"Mom wouldn't like it either," she continues citing the faults of my awesome idea. "What about the guests? Would you fly all of them, pay for the accommodations and their expenses?"

Well, I can't argue with that. I shrug. She smiles and looks back at the horizon. "I think either here or the Mountain View Terrace.

So, we're back to planning *the event*. "What are you thinking?"

She hums. "I think the Mountain View Terrace would be perfect at sunset. Especially if we take this place up on that discount for doing Friday morning instead of that evening or Saturday."

That sounds reasonable. "Okay, but will her royal obnoxiousness, Princess Charlie, agree to that?"

Eileen snorts. "As long as it looks amazing on her Instagram account, I'm sure she'll agree to that."

She seems so sure of herself. But with all the bullshit we've been through and all the crap her sister's put her through, I don't want us to fuck this up.

"But is this the place?" I ask earnestly.

She looks around for a bit. Her eyes comb over every inch of this place so meticulously.

"What do you think?" I ask again, while she studies the landscape and compares it with the pictures.

She stands in the middle of the gazebo and looks left, then right, toward the mountains.

"Does it make you want to say I do?" she asks curiously.

I shake my head. "There's nothing that would make me stand up in front of a bunch of people and say 'I do.'"

Again, I don't say.

"So, a smaller setting?" She doesn't even look at me as she talks. She's admiring the mountain view. "This isn't *too* big. They said up to a hundred and thirty guests. We don't have to invite everyone to the ceremony. We'll take whatever they have for the reception."

It's still too many people, I think.

She turns back to me as if reading my fucking mind. "You're being weirdly quiet. Still deciding about your ideal wedding?"

Instead of responding, I ask a question of my own. "Does this place make *you* want to tie your life to another person?"

She squints, craning her neck to look up at me. For a few beats, she remains quiet.

"I don't know if this is the place," she answers. "First I'd need the right guy. I'm not getting married to just *anyone*."

"So, you're still looking for *him*?"

She turns to look at me and flashes the smile she has on her face so fucking often. There's such tenderness in those eyes. Her face, and that smile, just soothes me.

"I'm too busy to get a haircut let alone date someone who isn't worth my time," she says with a soft voice. "But you know, I wouldn't marry someone just because of a broken condom."

"Like your sister," I say what she's trying to avoid.

She shrugs.

"I look at her and Marek, and I'm just not feeling it" she says, taking the scene in one more time before walking toward me. "Wouldn't you want to organize the most important day of your life?"

"I think they're busy trying to score a house," I say, knowing they were with Jack and Emmeline earlier today.

Marek is visiting everyone who would be willing to listen to him. I just don't think he'll find what Charlie is looking for. A brand new four-bedroom home—free of charge.

"When I find a guy worth shit," Eileen says. "I don't want to be worried about a wedding or where we're going to live."

The air is thin here. It goes well with the crisp afternoon air. Eileen is cool but calloused when it comes to love. I wonder if it's a family trait and she's just a gold digger.

So, I prod a little. "What if he can only afford a studio, doesn't have a car, and can't afford to pay for the wedding of your dreams?"

"Maybe that's why fifty percent of marriages end up in divorce," she answers. "People get married all the time for all the wrong reasons. You do it because you've come to realize that someone cares enough to see your bullshit and love you anyway. If you're too concerned about her looks, her job, where she lives... you're wasting your time."

She sighs. "I don't think that many weddings are about love. They're a convoluted status symbol. If you want it so badly, just elope."

My eyebrows shoot up. Well fuck, I wasn't expecting that. "What if you *can* afford the wedding of your dreams?"

She gives me an impish smile. "Then, I'll think about inviting a few people and do something small. Ten, fifteen people from each side of the family. You seem like the kind of guy that would let her do everything, and pay for it. You like to please people."

Now she's analyzing me. *Sweetheart, you don't know me at all.*

"And why the fuck would I do that?" I ask defensively.

That last statement doesn't sit well. We don't know each other, and she just assumes—not that she's wrong about it.

"Middle child," she responds. "We have the tendency to make everyone happy, right?"

Well, she got me there, didn't she?

"Maybe I would help her organize it." I let my gaze wander around anywhere but in her direction. "I'm here, aren't I?"

"Come on," she says inviting me to stand right by the gazebo. "Let's try this out."

"Try it?"

"Duh, we need to test drive this place." She extends her hand wiggling her fingers as she calls me to her. "What do you think?"

I take her hand. It's warm. Her grip soft, yet firm. She feels so familiar. I don't know what it is that I'm waiting for as I stand right in front of her. She squeezes my hand, kinda like she's saying "chill the fuck out."

Reluctantly, I take a deep breath. This place smells like pine with hints of hazelnut and cherry? Warm and bright, just like her. Her eyes stare at me curiously. Then, she nudges me to stare at the horizon again.

"Could you?" she whispers with a chuckle. "Doesn't it make you want to fall stupidly in love?"

The sky goes on forever. Just like her laugh. My breath catches. I almost forgot what it's like being up here, waiting for something that'll never come to pass.

I swallow thickly, terrified of how she made my heart beat faster. "Yeah."

12

Jason

Twelve days until the wedding

"I UNDERSTAND, THANKS," I grumble as I hang up on yet another wedding planner.

Deep breaths, I tell myself. Jossie cut me off after two espressos this morning so I'm left nursing a pitiful, decaf latte.

This ranks top of the list of "shittiest ways to spend my morning." I'm scrambling for a new wedding planner. I asked Jossie for help, but she has too much *real work* to entertain my personal affairs. If she wasn't such a life savior, I'd be firing her sassy ass right about now.

Charlie's friend is charging us double because we canceled on her yesterday. The ones I've called either laugh in my face or ask me for more money than the entire wedding budget combined. Maybe, I should just go ahead and pay them.

I really just want out of this fucking mess. Weddings are my kryptonite, and no one seems concerned about my well-being. My last resource is my younger brother, Alex. He might take pity on me and take over this mess.

"What can I do for you?" he says cheerfully after the first ring.

Have I mentioned how much I hate morning people?

"Why am I the one dealing with a fucking wedding?" I ask instead of greeting him. "Shouldn't it be June, Jeannette, or you?"

"Sure, throw your kid brother under the bus," he says.

"Better you than me."

"You skipped Jackson," he complains. "And Emmeline is the queen of organization. This would be right up her alley."

I sigh as I go back to googling "cheap wedding planners near me." I have another tab open with the search results for "how to bail out of a wedding you agreed to pay for," a third one with "how to not fall into the web of sweet, cute, sister-of-the-bride" and "how to make yourself repulsive to someone else."

"She offered to help me with a few things," I tell him. "But they're both out of the country for the next week. If not, I would've added them to the mix. Or better yet, shoved this off to them."

"Just stop enabling Marek," he says. "I never saw you do that for me when I had my accident."

Last year, he was in a car accident. At some point, the doctors mentioned that he wouldn't walk again. His X-game career ended that day. He walks with a limp, and I swear that I tried to be there for him. But he really didn't need me as much.

"You had Mom and the girls fussing all over you," I remind him. Our sisters mothered him to death while he was recovering. "The point is, I can't do this. Everyone knows it and no one fucking cares."

"We care, but you should be over it," he says. And then the fucker asks, "Do I really have to be there for the big day? We know how this is going to turn out, don't we?"

"And they say I'm the cynic of this family," I respond, resigned that this asshole isn't going to help me.

This isn't worth my time. Marek won't even appreciate it. It's just going to be yet another disaster wedding I've lived through. And an unhappy marriage I have to witness. Until he asks for money to pay for a divorce lawyer.

"What do you need help with?" he asks in a resigned tone.

"Just about everything," I answer. "Fuck. I'm sick of all of it. Bridezilla is so fucking incompetent. Marek isn't any better. And don't get me started on this fucking chick—"

"There's a chick involved?" he asks, amusement in his voice.

"Yeah," I say. "Sister of the Bride."

"So, she's hot?"

I think about it for a second. Sure, Eileen's pretty. Her voice is sweet but confident. She's fucking smart as shit and has a mouth to match. She's cool but not in an obnoxious know-it-all kinda way. She's hilarious and charismatic.

Sometimes I catch myself holding my breath when she watches me. She gets this look on her face sometimes like she's waiting for me to spill my guts. I feel as if she can read my mind and even touch my soul with her sweet gaze.

I had to stop myself a couple of times yesterday from telling her my walrus joke. Last night, I wanted to hear her voice before I fell asleep. And I almost called her this morning to say maybe I should bail on planning this wedding. Hoping she'll convince me otherwise.

I never call women. Well, except for Jossie—but she doesn't count.

"Uh ,you know," I say casually. "I don't think so... haven't really had time to get a good look at—"

"Wow, you've got it bad," Alex declares as if he knows better than I do.

There's a knock at the door. I check the monitor. The first thing I spot is that bright smile and those crinkly green eyes. She makes me smile against my better judgment as I open the door.

"Uh, I gotta go," I tell Alex.

"Let me guess, it's *her*," he says flatly.

"Yeah, sounds great," I say as I hang up on him.

"It's you," I say, as I usher her in. "How did you know where I live?"

"Marek told me," she explains walking into my house and looking around. "I thought it was easier to come over than go to my parents' house to make a call."

I stare at her dumbfounded. This is the last place I expected to see her. In my house. How can I avoid her if she just saunters into my domain looking all hot with those skinny jeans and the loose white blouse?

"Do you know there are really no payphones anymore?" she asks.

Payphones?

What is she talking about? I blink twice rewinding the conversation. What did I miss?

Was she going to call me?

"How did you get my number?" I question. "And more importantly, where the fuck is your phone?"

"Charlie and Marek paid me an early visit," she clarifies.

I check the time, nine in the morning—what the fuck is wrong with people? It's too early for a Sunday morning.

"I can't find my phone," she continues. "The last time I saw it was when we went to dinner. It might be in your car, honestly."

"How about the restaurant?"

She shakes her head. "I already went there."

"You know there's an app for that," I joke.

She nods. I barely catch the smirk she gives me. "Can we check your car just to make sure I didn't leave it there? I think it's dead. It keeps going to voicemail."

"You're wrong but, sure," I say as I grab my keys and put on my shoes. "You hungry? I was thinking about grabbing something."

"My fridge is empty," I lie.

She scrunches her nose and says, "I could use a coffee."

As we walk to the elevator, she tells me, "Charlie forced me to make decaf this morning so she wouldn't 'smell caffeine' in case it's bad for her kid or whatever. It was gross and sad, let's leave it at that."

"A woman after my own heart," I declare.

She nudges me with her elbow, laughing. She laughs even harder when we find her phone in the center console of my car.

"Told you so," she says triumphantly.

"Guess I owe you a real coffee," I offer.

"You already owed me that," she reminds me with an unamused face. "Never play with my caffeine."

"Fine," I concede, "Name your price."

She hums looking at me thoughtfully as I turn on the car. Why does she keep doing that? Do I have something on my face?

"I'll come up with something," she says finally.

13

Jason

I TAKE her to this brunch place in the city. It's your standard, gentrified restaurant with exposed brick and too much industrial metal and random wildflowers. To hipster for my taste. But it does have some great biscuits and some of the best coffee blends.

She makes a big fuss about their menu.

"Peach cobbler waffles with ice cream for breakfast," she says looking at the picture menu. "I regret ordering the double chocolate fudge pancakes."

"You like your sweets, don't you?"

Eileen smiles at me. She swipes some foam off the top of her latte, lapping it up with a moan. She moans a little louder when she takes her first sip.

That's it, she's trying to kill me. She not only looks beautiful today, but those noises she's making are making me think all kinds of naughty thoughts. I should keep my thoughts out of the gutter when it comes to her.

Guilt claws at me when I think about what could happen if we hooked up. She's about to become part of the family. We are also sort of friends. Eileen is off limits. I have standards, rules, and limits. I can't be bedding some chick I'll be seeing at the next family reunion.

Yet, here we are, eating brunch and hanging out like two people who are getting to know each other — even—flirting. I should stop doing that just about now. Treat her like my sister. I look at her and she's nothing like June or Jeannette.

How about Emmeline?

"I think I'm addicted to caffeine," she suddenly confesses, and I smile.

A woman after my own heart. *You're perfect,* I think.

I raise my cup to her. "Guess that makes two of us."

She smirks, reaching over the table. What the fuck is she—

"Here," she says as she swipes some foam from my cup before sticking it in my face. "I think you've—"

"What are you doing—" I try to dodge her, futilely.

She gets me right on the lip. My skin is warm from the sizzle of her touch. I have a hard time thinking, and I'm craving more of that warmth.

"Yeah, see? You've got something on your face," she says with a lopsided grin.

A fucking foam mustache. Why didn't I think of that?

Well, two can play at this game.

"Oh no, you seem to have something too," I say as I grab some foam from my cup. "Let me help with that."

"Nope, nuh-uh," she protests lightly as she leans back.

"I insist," I say.

She dodges well enough for me to miss her upper lip but not her forehead. Her breath catches. The sound tightens my chest. And I retrieve my hand out of fear because I want to run my finger across her gorgeous face, trace a line on her long, beautiful neck and follow it with my lips.

But the playful atmosphere changes radically.

Eileen is quiet now that she's sporting a coffee foam unibrow and a scowl. For a second, I'm worried I've pushed the wrong button and she's going to murder me, but for real. She uses her crappy phone camera to get a look at herself.

"Wow, you got me good," she says with a laugh. "I'm impressed."

"Yeah?" I ask hesitantly, afraid that she can hear my thoughts and guess my needs.

"Yeah," she says with a soft smile. "Let's hope your taste in music is as good as your sense of humor."

I think my heart forgets to work for a second. I can't think straight, so I go with what I know best—that goddamn sense of humor.

"You wish your taste in music was as good as mine," I say, waggling my eyebrows suggestively.

She rolls her eyes with a smile that tells me she gets it. Yep, I can safely say this woman is going to be the death of me if I don't raise my walls.

But do I want to do it?

"So, you like coffee, sugar, and beer," I conclude. "What else is there to know about Eileen McBean?"

She's quiet as the waitress sets up our breakfast. "Would you like another latte?"

"Another round for both," I order and thank her as she leaves.

"It's not beer," Eileen says, and then she does it again. Another long moan as she takes the first bite of her pancakes.

Fuck. If she sounds like that while eating, how does she sound when she's making love? My dick threatens to break a few rules. My mind is doing the same. A woman like her is priceless. One of a kind and—what would I give to find out more about Eileen? Not just in bed, but...

Stop, I order myself.

She shoots over a smile and says, "You haven't touched your food."

I stare at her like a teenager crushing for the first time.

Be strong, Spearman.

The fear of doing something stupid, like throw caution to the wind, makes me dig deep into the memories. Because I know this story. It starts as fun and games, but in the end, one of us will be waiting for something that'll never happened.

Hell if I'll let that happen to me again.

14

Eileen

IS he actively trying to ruin my life?

Okay, he's hot, I get it. Tall, mind-blowing body and handsome as fuck. And he isn't a soulless, rich demon like Charlie made him out to be.

But does he have to be funny?

Why can't he be a boring, awkward nerd?

The fact that he can listen to me talking with attention is making it ridiculously hard to breathe sometimes. If not every second I'm with him. Sorting through my thoughts is close to impossible.

We're organizing a wedding. As much as I'm trying to suppress romantic thoughts for this guy I barely know, they keep popping out from left and right. I try to keep the mood light, but now it's up to auditioning bands.

What am I going to do if they play a slow, cheesy song?

I try to keep the mood light, but now it's up to auditioning bands. What am I going to do if they play a slow, cheesy song?

Where did he even get bands and DJs to audition?

"What do you do for a living?" I ask as he parks in front of the hotel.

"Does it matter?" he asks before opening his door.

No, but where do the luxury cars come from? Last Saturday was a Ferrari. Then, on Sunday a Bugatti, and today we're riding in a fancy Audi which model I've never seen before. Now he has this place set within short notice.

Who are you?

The valet opens my door and helps me down, but in seconds Jason is next to him taking away my hand from the man. Great, now he's going to see what a sweaty idiot I can be.

"Not really," I answer. "Just asking because you somehow have a place ready with bands who are willing to audition for you."

"For *us*," he clarifies. "Plus, DJs too."

"Okay, but bands and DJs on such short notice?"

He shrugs. "I wish I could take credit for the setup, but it was Emmeline."

Well, that's new. That little piece of information takes care of any romantic thoughts I might be harboring. He has a significant other.

I flash him a questioning look. "Your girlfriend?" *Wife, partner... this proves that all the good ones are taken.*

"Fuck no, my oldest brother's girlfriend," he says emphatically.

Somehow the revelation eases the tension in my back. Why do I care if he's otherwise occupied by a beautiful woman? It's none of my business.

But he's so funny, and thoughtful, and smart. That goofy personality that he keeps hidden underneath the serious guy is breathtaking.

Easy there, girl. He's just an acquaintance helping me with Charlie's latest 'emergency'.

"So, I assume we don't like Emmeline."

"She's... good for *Jack*," he states a little thoughtfully. "Kind of a fucking busy body, but she gets shit done and doesn't take shit from *him*."

I snort. "You don't know anything about her."

"Do too," he says.

"Name one thing you like about her personally."

"Easy, she makes a mean espresso," he says. "But she's a pain in my ass, and her cats are demons."

"What's wrong with cats?" I say defensively.

"Nothing, I love cats," he says. "Hers just ruined my brother's sweet decor."

"Ah, personal vendetta," I joke, but glance at him wondering how their relationship affected his own. "Let me guess, she took away your brother's attention."

He bumps my hip lightly with his, giving me a tight smile. Ding, ding. I hit the jackpot. "The spot for best friend is open, in case..." He goes silent, and I love his bashfulness.

I think about Camilla and how it'd be to lose our time together because she finds love. That brings me to thinking about Jason and how much I enjoy being with him. I glance at him again, wondering if in another life where there are no shotgun weddings and I was a little more put together, we could've been something else.

Thankfully he doesn't look my way, or he'd see how hard I'm blushing.

As we enter the ballroom, there's a small stage where instruments are already set up. In front of the stage, there are two chairs with a small table between them.

"We'll have dinner served for two while we enjoy the music," he says.

This wasn't a part of my schedule. "Part of the catering selection?"

"No, just dinner," he says. "I hope you don't mind. I just order bites."

"Bites?"

"Appetizers. You know, pretzels, nachos, hummus, pita, and beer, of course."

"Oh, bar food," I say excitedly. "Sure, that's like my comfort food."

"What?" He does a double take.

His brows crease. It makes me want to smooth out his face with my thumb.

"My dad's Irish, remember?" I explain. "He owned a pub with one of his brothers while I was growing up, and I ate a lot of bar food."

"What happened to it?" he asks.

"They sold it and then Dad decided to become an electrician. He says it pays better. I wouldn't know."

"Doing what you love doesn't always pay well," he says thoughtfully.

"Preaching to the choir, pal," I say.

He starts to reach over with his hand, but the server comes out with two beers. I'm relieved because it looked like he was trying to reach over and squeeze my arm. But I'm *disappointed* because it looked like he was trying to reach over and squeeze my arm.

"So, what kind of music does the bride and the groom want to listen to during their big day?" he asks instead.

"I have a list of songs that my parents would like the band to play, but most of the stuff it's just, you know, commercial pop that Charlie wants."

His nose moves slightly. It's not a scrunch, but I can tell he isn't thrilled about the music selection.

"Well, what would you prefer to listen to? Heavy metal in the middle of your wedding reception?"

"Jazz," he says. "I'll take some Post-Bop or smooth jazz but, I don't know, weddings seem like the best time for a swing band. You know what I mean?"

I perk up, dumbfounded. Charlie always called me a weirdo for caring about Jazz.

"Yeah," I say, clearing my throat. "I honestly couldn't agree more.

Although it would probably be easier to find a band that does Retro Swing covers of pop music. Keep the theatricality and sound of Swing but make the music selection more recent and accessible. That way everyone would be happy."

Jason gets this goofy grin every so often. Like he has no idea what he's doing, but he's just so excited about something. It's adorable. It makes me excited to be around him and whatever's making him so happy.

He has seven bands and eight DJs lined up. The DJs perform first because it's easier to spot the best one. When the bands start playing, there are some really good performances and others ... let's just say I'm hoping for this last number to be over.

Once they finish, the next band begins to play Jazz. Jason rises from his seat, he extends his hand and says, "May I have this dance?"

Without thinking, I accept enthusiastically. I have no idea how this will turn out. He moves at a perfect pace. He's so graceful and dashing. His eyes pierce me. A rush of heat sweeps down my chest as we move around the dance floor.

"You're pretty good at this," he says, lightening the intensity of the moment with a chuckle.

"You're not too bad yourself, sir," I say playfully.

He turns to the band, "Do you take requests?"

The singer of the band nods. Jason looks at me mischievously before he walks up to the stage and whispers something into her ear. The singer says something to the band and counts them in. They start playing an all too familiar hook.

"Fuck no," I say.

"Come on, Eileen," he sings, offering me his hand with a shit eating grin.

"Nope," I say stubbornly.

"Come on, *Eileen*, you know you want to," he says.

"You're awful," I say as I take his hand.

His dancing should be illegal. He's sweeping me off my feet, literally. He picks me up so smoothly for a turn.

"Come on, Eileen," he sings in harmony with the band's singer.

I laugh. "Don't think I'm enjoying this."

He dips me.

"Wouldn't dream of it," he says.

I get lost in the way he leads us around the dance floor.

"Come on, Eileen," he sings along with the band and as much as I'm trying to be upset this is so much fun.

He dips me again. His face is so close to mine, I could just lean up and kiss him.

I blush, my heart threatening to jump out of my chest. "You skipped a few lines."

"Admit it," he says, ignoring me as he takes me out of the dip. "You've always wanted to have a big party, just for you."

How does he know this shit about me?

"Middle child, remember?" he says sadly.

I wish he didn't get me. It would make pushing him away easier. It would make keeping all of this casual, professional, easy.

"I admit that I wanted to experience something like this. With a better dress, of course, and maybe a few more guests. You know, like in those teen movies."

"Didn't they have live music during your school dances?" he asks.

"Once, during my senior prom. But I didn't go."

"How come you didn't?"

I shrug. "It was my birthday."

"You must have done something pretty fun instead of going to a boring school dance."

I laugh, maybe a bit hysterically. "Not really."

15

Eileen

Nine Years Ago: Eileen's Eighteenth Birthday

I SET my pen down on the paper as the teacher says, "Your time is up." My hand is shaking too much, but I think I got everything right. I inhale a few calming breaths, attempting to calm my nerves.

"It's over," I remind myself internally. "Your last AP test ever."

I pick up the test and hand it over to the teacher as she walks through the desks collecting the tests.

Another teacher barges in, saying, "Eileen McBean, report to the office with your things. Your parents are waiting for you."

Camilla turns to look at me and frowns. We're supposed to go to her house after school. Since my parents are busy today, I'm celebrating my birthday with her and her family.

Tomorrow, we're getting mani-pedis, and then we're going to prom. At least, that's the plan. I shrug as I glance at her and grab my things. When I arrive at the principal's office, my parents are waiting for me. What is this?

"What happened?"

"We've decided to take a trip to Los Angeles," my mother says with a tight smile.

I pinch myself. This must be a dream. My parents are usually too busy to celebrate my birthday, let alone take me on a trip.

"You're kidding? This is really happening?" I say excitedly.

Best surprise birthday present ever!

I throw myself at Mom and hug her tight. "We're really going on that trip for my birthday just like you promised?"

When I look up at them, I notice that they look at each other slightly confused. But immediately they both say, "Of course, your birthday trip."

Things start crumbling as soon as we pick up Sam from school. My brother insists we eat at the Shack before we go to the airport, but there's not enough time for that. Mom promises to grab something before we board the plane.

After going through airport security, we head to one of the restaurants that serves seafood. Sam insists on getting the shrimp and scallops ultimate plate.

"That's a lot of food for an eleven-year-old boy," the lady next to us says. "We have a kids' menu. How about some popcorn shrimp?"

Mom glares at her. Of course, how dare someone tells her how to raise her children. Mom also is a little passive-aggressive. So instead of saying anything, she asks for not one, but two ultimate plates to go.

"He's a growing boy," she says to the cashier.

"I want—"

"You'll share the food with him," Mom whispers.

Great. I get to eat seafood over the juicy bacon cheeseburger that I wanted. The joy of being the middle child. Once we're on the plane and Mom hands us the food, Sam refuses to eat it.

"It's cold," he protests, her shoulders slumping.

He wasn't really hungry. Brat. I'm not thrilled about it but devour mine.

Regardless, I try to stay strong. My parents never think of me first. I never thought they would actually take me out for my birthday. I spend the entire plane ride listening to the cheesiest glam rock and 80s pop hits, dreaming of a weekend of sun, fun, and maybe even boys?

The rental car isn't great, but it'll get the four of us to the beach. I wonder if Charlie's going to meet us somewhere. She lives here now. I don't see why she'd miss my birthday if she's already here.

My parents keep looking over their shoulder every so often as I tell them where I'd like to go. The beach, shopping, Hollywood... everything.

"And will you be staying here for business or pleasure?" The concierge asks during our check-in.

I smile triumphantly, answering for my parents, "Pleasure. It's my eighteenth birthday."

I ignore my brother making puking noises next to me, and how Mom sighs quietly next to me. I don't even think about how my mom whispers, "Great, now we're going to have to stay the whole weekend," to my dad as we pass the elevator to our first-floor rooms.

Once we're settled in the room, my dad says, "You two stay here."

"Where are you going?" I ask confused.

"We have to check on Charlie," he admits sheepishly.

Okay, fine, but... "What are we doing later today?"

"Dinner, maybe cake," my mom responds quickly. "We should walk through Rodeo Drive."

I'm really excited, but my stomach feels uneasy. Maybe some motion sickness from the landing or maybe it's the putrid smell of smog. When my parents close the door, the nausea increases, clawing at my throat.

I run toward the bathroom. Chunks of partially digested food spew out of my coughing, choking mouth. My stomach contracts violently, forcing everything up and out. I'm sweating and in tears. I lurch forward and sink to my knees.

When my parents return from visiting my sister, it's almost midnight. I'm still right next to the toilet.

My dad gives me a worried look as he enters the bathroom. "Are you okay, sweetie?"

"No," I say, glaring at him.

"She's been puking all night," Sam complains, disgusted. "If you were planning on paying her for babysitting, I'd think twice."

As if they ever pay me.

I watch Dad nodding out of the corner of my eye. "I'll find you some crackers."

At the mention of food, I puke again.

Unfortunately, the weekend isn't any different. I'm stuck in a hotel room, sick and babysitting my brother. It isn't until we were driving through Nevada a few days later—with a cramped car full of Charlie's shit—that I find out my sister was kicked out of school three months ago and had just run out of money. They were here to pick her up. Once again, I was a fucking afterthought.

Happy birthday, Eileen.

At least this is better than my not-so-sweet sixteen.

16

Eileen

Eleven Years ago: Eileen's Sixteen Birthday

"WHAT ARE YOU GUYS DOING TODAY?" Camilla asks over the phone.

I shrug, but obviously she can't see me, so I answer. "I honestly don't know. Are you sure they didn't organize a surprise party?"

They did that for Charlie's sweet sixteen. Instead of a fancy party like she requested, they decided to throw her a surprise party with all her friends. The cake was pink with unicorns. They also gave her money for a trip with her bestie, Amanda.

The last part is what quieted the temper tantrum she had going when she realized that they hadn't booked a ballroom or had a luxury car parked by the garage.

"Sorry, Eileen, if your parents organized it, they forgot to invite me."

"Typical," I say, scrunching my nose.

"Mom says to head over. She has a surprise for you," Camilla announces. "If they let you, you can stay over."

I look outside the window and spot my dad's car. He's parking by the driveway.

"Tell her thank you," I say. "Dad's here, and he has a box on the bed of the truck."

"Call if you need me," she says before hanging up.

———

EARLIER TODAY, DAD BOUGHT A NEW BICYCLE FOR MY BROTHER. His old one was stolen last week. As he tried his bike, I waited for Dad to unload his truck. Maybe they didn't plan a party, but he hinted something about a new car.

At least I think that's what he meant when he said, "Everyone has to have a set of wheels."

I hope we go and check out Mrs. Johnson's old car later this evening or tomorrow afternoon. Would this be it?

My stomach feels uneasy. What if this is yet another disastrous birthday? In all honesty, he hasn't promised to buy me a car for my sixteenth birthday. Yeah, but I've been hinting that I had some money saved up, and if they matched the thousand dollars, I could buy my first new car.

"What are we doing today?" I asked Dad casually.

"I'm not sure honey. Why don't you ask your mom," he answers preoccupied.

Two can play at this game. "She's still at work," I say innocently.

"Well, let's wait for her and see what she wants to do."

I smile, going along with his ruse. He's doing such a great job of playing dumb. They must have something really good planned for my birthday. Probably something to make up for the disaster of last year's birthday dinner... or the wasp's nest that ruined the year before that.

Maybe they've organized a surprise birthday party for me, and Camilla played dumb?

"Watch out shit-for-breath!" my brother shouts.

I turn around a second too late. His bike crashes into me, forcing my body to slam right against Dad's truck. This is only the fourth most painful day of my life, sadly.

An hour later, I found myself at the ER getting X-rays. This is apparently cutting into Mom's knitting club, which is something every girl wants to hear on her birthday. Did she forget my birthday?

I'm not going to cry; I'm not going to cry.

My throat is clogged with tears. I'm not sure if it's the pain or the hurt that my mother finds me forgettable.

"Why couldn't you be more careful, Eileen?" Mom chides me as she arrives in the emergency room.

My lip quivers. I can't believe she's not asking if I'm okay or says *fucking happy birthday.*

"You filled out all the information, Mr. McBean. You just forgot a few things," the nurse states as she's looking at the form.

Then, she looks at me. "Date of birth?"

"May twenty seventh," I mumble under my breath.

She smiles and says, "We have a birthday girl. Happy Birthday! How old are you?"

"Sixteen," I grumble.

"I bet you have a big party planned," she says cheerfully and then looks at my leg. "We might have to cancel the first dance."

I glance at my parents who are both red and staring at each other. They look at me like kicked puppy dogs. Great. They forgot, and now they feel guilty, so I have to pretend it's okay.

Happy fucking birthday, Eileen.

"I'm sorry, honey," Dad says when the nurse leaves. "I promise to make it up to you when you're better."

Is he ever going to make it up for every time he forgets I'm here?

17

Jason

Ten days until the wedding

"YES, Aunt Stacey... no, of course not," Eileen says as she looks over at me frantically. "Well, we've been planning this wedding for a while now so if you haven't received your invite yet, it must have been lost in the mail... Yeah, that's right. Our post office did a ton of layoffs a few months back."

She grimaces to me. I respond by scrunching up my nose until I make that "dumb, ugly face" Jossie likes to complain about. Eileen sticks her tongue out at me. So obviously I roll up mine in a hot dog shape at her. For added effect, I go cross-eyed at the same time.

Eileen has to stifle a laugh. Score one for me.

She glares and then flashes an ominous smirk. Her face morphs into this bizarre turtle impression.

I fucking lose it, covering my mouth to keep my laugh from getting to her aunt's eardrums.

It's really weird seeing someone jumping through all these hoops to make their family happy. In this case, Eileen is doing the impossible to make her family think Charlie isn't a huge flake.

Who would put up with a hopeless charade like this for so long?

Maybe it's because Charlie's more responsible than Marek—or maybe Eileen didn't give up on Charlie in her teens like I did with Marek.

Sure. Alex thinks I enable the fuck out of our cousin. But it used to be a lot worse. Everyone in our extended family knows what a screw up he can be. All I had to do is call up a few relatives, say "Hey, Marek got a girl knocked up. You coming to the wedding?"

Of course, most of them said no. At least the ones who said yes asked if everyone knew it was a shotgun wedding.

"Why are we only getting back to you just now?" Eileen says.

"Busy, grace period, trusted you," I whisper-shout.

She rubs her temple, squeezing her eyes shut. "Honestly... we know how busy you get and wanted to give you a grace period to follow up. Charlie was pretty devastated this morning when she saw you hadn't RSVP'd yet."

Some murmuring comes from the other line. Eileen's cat, Max, saunters into the living room as she continues talking. Looks like he has a lot of fun living in this place. For as small as this one bedroom is, it's brimming with shit clinging to the walls and sculptures cluttering the floor.

Eileen doesn't seem to mind the way Max climbs on them, which is good since he seems to have absolutely no respect for the arts. It's cool, though. All of these pieces are quirky, kind of vintage, but there's something timeless in how messy yet elegant they try to be.

They all scream, "Eileen's so cool and thoughtful she doesn't realize how cool she is."

"Yeah, exactly," she says. "That's why I knew it'd be best to contact you personally."

Max walks past her, walking over to my side of this ancient couch. He sniffs my jeans, clearly deeming me as the superior petter in this abode, and rubs up against my leg. I scratch the top of his head lightly.

"Think nothing of it," Eileen says.

She glances down at Max, gesturing for me to pick him up. Welp, this is either a very friendly cat or the world's cruelest joke.

"Come here, Maximilian," I whisper as I pick him up.

He squeaks once but then settles into my lap.

"Yes, of course we understand. I'll send them your regards." Eileen groans when she hangs up.

"Five down, only a thousand more to go," I say, kind of mockingly. "Keep it going, champ. I'll bring dinner if we need to stay here that long."

Eileen snorts. "You fucking cheated."

"How?" I say indignantly.

"You told your family the truth," she says.

"Uh, duh," I say. "Rule number one of the Spearmans—what's our business stays our business. Anyone else is fair game."

She yawns as she stretches. I get a flash of her plump tits as she bends down. My fingers crave to caress them.

God, what would it be to... Yep, totally normal, nothing to see here. One, three, seven, eleven, seventeen, twenty-three—

"Pretty sure yesterday you said," she interrupts my countdown to argue. 'Rule number one of the Spearman's is never give away your last donut unless someone has an espresso to compensate you.'"

"We have a lot of first rules," I claim. "That was the first rule of donuts."

"Nice save," she says.

She gets up from her seat with a sigh.

"I'm tired," she confesses and asks, "Are you tired? We should just give up and tell Charlie everyone canceled."

"Great idea," I prompt and arch an eyebrow. "However... and just bear with me for a second. Have you considered how she'll hunt all of these people down to personally apologize to her?"

"You *are* a fast learner," she concedes with a groan. "Want something to lighten the mood? I've got shitty beer and cheap wine."

"Beer me," I say.

As she walks away my eyes trail after her. Her curly hair bounces as her hips sway languidly toward the kitchen. Her sweats do a perfect job of framing that luscious ass of hers. Does she work hard to always look so put together and gorgeous?

Or does she just roll out of bed like that?

She's gorgeous.

What the fuck, Spearman. *Rule number one of being Jason Spearman. You don't develop crushes.*

I shake my head, slapping myself a little. Nope, strictly platonic acquaintance shit happening here. Nothing out of the ordinary. Think about something else. Mom, June, Jeannette. I sigh, knowing they would adore Eileen. Come on, if they can keep up with Emmeline, I don't see why they can't add... There I go again.

"Hey, uh, why don't we take a break? Watch TV or something," I suggest trying to keep my mind busy.

"Alright, but I don't have cable," she announces.

"Who has cable these days?" I retort. "We could stream something?"

She points at the chest under the mounted screen. "I've got DVDs and bootlegged musicals."

I must be dreaming. "Holy fuck. Which ones?"

"*Rent, Wicked, 25th Annual Putnam County Spelling Bee...*" she says as she passes me a beer and sits down with her glass of wine. "I think I loaned my copy of *The Drowsy Chaperone* to Camilla, my best friend. But I should also have *Spring Awakening, Waitress,* and *If/Then.*"

Marry me, I think. *You're perfect.*

"How are you literally the coolest person I know," I say without thinking.

She giggles. "You know most people don't hear *musicals* and say *that's cool.*"

"Most people think slapping glitter on their face makes them look cool," I inform her.

"Hey now," she says with a straight face. Hands on her hips and murderous eyes. "I may have to reconsider your stay here if you have a problem with glitter."

I shrug, petting Max behind the ear. "Your cat has no problem with me and my snobbery."

"Yes, but he also thinks you, and everything else in this apartment, is a couch," she says, bursting my bubble. I glare at the cat. *I thought we became fast friends.*

"Besides," she continues. "He doesn't care about being friends with the *cool kids.*"

"What a coincidence. Neither do I."

Eileen shakes her, head taking a sip of her wine. While we choose what to watch, it confuses me how comfortable I feel in her place, with her company. I don't mind Max being on my lap.

What does this mean?

That we're friends, or that I haven't built tall enough walls to avoid the attraction that continues to grow between us.

I should just leave.

18

Jason

SINCE WHEN DID I stop listening to my own advice?

I stay, and then, I talk Eileen into watching the Lion King marathon. She even owns one called *The Lion King* 1½. Who knew that existed?

We stay quiet as the movie begins, but I can only do that for so long. Who doesn't like to sing along? This is one of the best Disney movies *ever* because of the songs.

"You're so dramatic," she says later as I lift Max up like Rafiki does to Simba... for the fifth time.

"I have no idea what you're talking about," I tell her. "I'm just a lowly amateur performer, starving for applause."

She stares blankly for a moment. Shit, what does that expression mean? I'm just fucking around in my future cousin-in-law's sister's apartment and it's weird now. I can't remember the last time someone left one of my jokes hanging, let alone left me hanging with stress sweats.

What is this?

"Amateur, huh?" she says carefully. "I've never heard an amateur put that much power into *Hakuna Matata*."

I shrug, putting Max on the floor and out of his misery. Taking a swig of beer, I sit down next to her. We watch in silence for a while. It doesn't matter what she thinks. It doesn't matter how I sing or where I do it.

Who fucking cares?

I don't even know what she's thinking.

"Why does it matter?" Fine, I do care what she thinks about me.

"Say what now, Pumba?" she says dryly.

"Who cares if I'm an amateur?" I argue.

"No one," she says slowly. "I was just thinking... a guy like you—"

I take a look at myself and frown. "Like what?"

"Rich, conventionally attractive, with a decent set of pipes." She lists out my attributes on one hand. "I don't see why you couldn't throw some money around, be semi-professional maybe?"

I smile grimly. "Would if I could."

"But you can't?"

"It's too late."

"Too late for what?"

"For—" I sigh in frustration. "I don't owe you my tragic backstory, alright?"

There's nothing tragic about not going into acting. I was decent at best. Do I love it? Yes, who doesn't love to get on stage and sing a few songs while pretending to be someone else. But as much as my parents supported my dreams, they also kept me grounded.

"Jason, do what you love, but also what you are good at," Dad told me after the twentieth failed audition. I didn't get one single callback, and it was amateur theater.

In the end, I understood I was good. Not good enough to become Jonathan Gruff, Christian Bale, Gary Oldman, Neil Patrick-Harris or Jeremy Jordan. Maybe it was somehow tragic when I was eighteen, but I'm over it.

Eileen stares at me blankly... again. This is getting on my fucking nerves. Why doesn't she just say what she's thinking?

"Okay," she says a million years later.

That's it? "Okay what?"

"Just... okay. You're right," she says. "I was just curious if you knew how good you are."

Well that's—something.

I squirm in my seat. These couch cushions are so fucking uncomfortable.

We're so quiet I barely remember to recite all the lines in the third act. Eileen's so... confusing. It's like she sees right through every single joke with some special X-ray vision and calls me out on some of my shit, but also doesn't? I don't get her.

"Didn't you have something you wanted to be when you were a kid?" I say, apropos of nothing.

"Sure," she agrees without giving any context.

"Wouldn't you have done anything in the world to become that?"

She nods, and I wait for her to tell me. Nothing.

"Well," I ask. "What is it?"

She takes a deep breath. "I guess when I was really young... but then, you know, I grew up. It doesn't pay the bills."

"Exactly," I say, unsatisfied by her answer but she has a point. "You have a dream. It gets destroyed by adulthood. You get used to disappointment. Reality settles and you move on. End of story."

"But what about now?" she insists. "Don't you have enough to pay your bills?"

"Not forever. Can't make a career out of a three-month vacation," I argue.

Or maybe I could if I really want to. Perhaps it's true what they say, you have to allow yourself to change your mind to be happy. And I can't say I'm happy, but I'm pretty close to content.

Clearly, she gives it some thought before toasting her drink against mine. "To stolen dreams, I guess."

The thought sinks in and simmers deep in my gut for a while. Did I give up on my dream? No, I talked it through. It wasn't relinquishing, more like finding something better. Was it? It just happened. Even if it kinda sucks.

"What was yours?" I ask eventually. "Uh, dream I mean."

"Muralist," she mumbles while she pours herself a second glass of wine. "We should order some food."

And that's— "Really? You?"

Her face turns red. "Loved to paint, wanted to be some... I don't know, social activist? Banksy, but less shitty I guess."

I laugh. She joins in and it's so fucking beautiful. And just like that, she stops, sighing deeply.

"What happened?" I question, reaching for her hand.

"My sister became an art major on a whim, didn't know how to do anything, but bullshitted her trash into this last-minute symposium on anti-capitalist structures."

She sighs. "With someone else's portfolio."

Charlie isn't smart enough for that. "So, she plagiarized your work," I guess.

"Yep," she confirms. "Then, they kicked her out of the program. Obviously, she ran out of money and forced my parents to come save her ass. They told me a week later they wouldn't pay for art school."

"Holy fucking—" I say. "How is your family that shitty?"

"You get used to it," she says.

Who does that to their sister? And who takes one kid's mistakes and punishes the other for it? What the fuck is wrong with these people?

I think I hate them just a little.

Worst of all, why can't she see how messed up that is?

If that were my family, I would've hashed shit out or walked out a long time ago. Then again, I'm not her. And though my parents aren't perfect, they are fucking great. I'm not judging, but come on, they could've done a lot better for Eileen.

I remember back when Marek was my best friend growing up. Before all the bullshit and lame excuses. I'd do anything for that kid, even if I could barely give a fuck about the guy he became. Wonder if Eileen's waiting on some version of Charlie that won't come back.

I nudge her shoulder. She looks up wearily.

"Hey kettle," I say lightly. "Wanna finish this movie and wallow in some more alcohol?"

"Only if you order some food," she responds.

At least she doesn't do that fake smile around me that I've seen thrown at her family around me. Her smile is sad but genuine. She's lively and funny without them, relaxed.

"Bar food, right?"

"Yeah, pot," she says. "I'd love that."

I hate to admit that this is by far one of the best nights I've had in a long time, but can it be sustainable? When will I fuck up?

19

Jason

I'D TAKE any kind or shape of Medieval torture instead of having to take part in this horrendous circus.

"No, no, fuck no!" Charlie screams.

Ouch, I'm losing my hearing with this woman.

"What is wrong with you people?!" she continues.

Charlie is as charming as fucking ever. Somehow, I naively thought wedding dress shopping was going to be easy. Instead, I've been sitting on a tiny love seat between Eileen and her mother for the last hour while Charlie... well, pulls *a Charlie.*

She clearly has telepathy, and knows I'm talking smack in my head because she chooses this moment to remember we exist, turns around on her pedestal in front of the mirror wall of this bridal boutique, and glare daggers at me.

"And you," she hisses. "I can't believe you accepted their champagne after I said the smell was irritating me."

What are you, a bloodhound? I want to be understanding with this woman but shit if she doesn't try her best to piss me off every five fucking minutes. Where is Marek when I need him to mediate the situation? Right, working. I should give him some props for finding a job.

Eileen and her mom tense on either side of me. Sure, normally this would be the part where Eileen jumps up and fixes shit. But I nudge her with my elbow before I shrug casually at Charlie.

"It's rude not to accept refreshments, Charlotte," I say with my charity events voice. "You'd do well to remember that. You know, for the future."

She blushes brightly as she subconsciously presses the wrinkles out of her latest dress. "Y-yes, of course."

Charlie turns back to the already frightened to death bridal consultant. "You still haven't shown me anything worth buying. What do you have to say for yourself?"

"Jeez," I say.

The glare from Charlie tells me I've pushing my fucking luck.

Eileen puts a hand on my knee. "Bless you," she says her eyes creeping in Charlie's direction.

Oh, this is my save. Cool. "Thank you," I say earnestly, wrinkling my nose.

It seems to be enough for her royal highness. She continues terrorizing the employees.

"I'll give you props for that first deflection," Eileen says quietly.

"And I'll thank you for the second one," I admit almost saying we're a great team.

"Don't thank me," she mumbles. "Find some way to get us out of here,"

I can do that, I think. I text Jossie "SOS."

A minute later, my phone starts playing *"Jossie's on a vacation far away—"*

"Is that seriously your ringtone?" Eileen asks. "The Outfield is a little outdated, even for you."

"Only for Jossie," I clarify. "Would you like to hear your ringtone?"

She chuckles and rolls her eyes, "Typical."

I ignore the scrutinizing glare her mother gives us as I pick up the call.

"Go for Spearman," I say as I stand up. "Excuse me, ladies—"

"No," Jossie says when I'm just out of earshot.

"I didn't even—" Too late, she's hung up on me.

I hate when she does this.

I call her. She picks up on the first ring.

"You're either trying to get out of wedding planning, which you can't, or trying to rope me into it," she says. "Which I won't."

"C'mon please, Jossie, please?" I beg her. "If anyone can save me from this shit show it's you."

"No, Jason," she says. "There's nothing you can say—"

"Two months' vacation," I list a few ways to convince her to step in just for a day. "What if I double your Christmas bonus this year, and you get paid like a wedding planner for this one teeny tiny task."

"Hmm," she says as if considering it.

"You have two minutes to talk," she says. "Go."

I take a deep breath. "This bride was bridezilla before she was even a person. Now she's bridezilla ultra-pregnancy edition, and all we're trying to do here is get a wedding dress. It's her sister, her mother, and me. They can't say no to her, and she hates me because I love saying no."

"And?" she prompts.

I grimace. "And I'll love you forever?"

"Ship's sailed on that."

"I'll..." What else could she want from me? "Give you the keys to the place in Miami for two weeks?"

"Wow, the house in Miami for the entire month of March next year?" she tweaks my offer. "Along with vacation pay during that month."

"You got it," I agree immediately.

There's a long pause. I check the phone to make sure she's still on the line.

"Sounds like a pickle, Mr. Spearman," she says dryly.

I groan. *"That's what I've been trying to say.* So, would you please, please, please get down to this boutique and talk her crazy language."

Jossie hums for a moment. "Alright. Let me make some calls, and I'll be right there."

"Perfe—and you hung up on me again," I say.

I pace back and forth, buying myself some time. There's no way I'm going back to listen to Charlie complain about every single thing that's wrong with the store and her poor luck.

"What's going on?" Eileen says as she finds me leaning against the front door of the shop. "You missed dresses seven and eight."

Thank fuck!

"I called my assistant for a, well, *assist* and she's coming to save our butts," I explain without adding that I was taking a Charlie break. "And guess what? She's taking mercy on us!"

Eileen scowls. "So, you called your executive assistant to... do what exactly?"

I perk up as I hear the sound of heels clicking against the pavement behind me.

"He contacted the best wedding planner he knows," Jossie, who is far from humble, says as she walks up to us with a to-go tray of coffee in her hands. "But not to fear, I've arrived."

Jossie shoves the tray toward me. "Jason, hold these."

"Yes, ma'am." I salute her before grabbing the drinks.

"Cappuccinos for you and the maid of honor," she explains. "Decaf-skinny-latte for the mother, and my special herbal tea ginger ale concoction for the bride."

"Are you psychic or just a miracle worker?" Eileen asks.

I bet she's as impressed as I am by the efficiency of this woman.

Jossie never ceases to amaze me, even though I've worked with her for years. She's more than a miracle worker.

Jossie offers Eileen her hand to shake. "Josslyn Udayar. I own Jason's life."

Eileen frowns giving me a questioning look. I answer with a shrug. Jossie doesn't own me, but I'm not sure what I'd do without her in my life.

"That means, I know where he is at all times," Jossie explains. "Which includes when he's not only completely out of his depth, but also when he's wasting my good wedding contacts that I have to salvage."

"Eileen McBean," Eileen offers with that soft genuine smile of hers. "I barely own my own life and apparently own my sister's."

Eileen looks over her shoulder and whispers, "Please save us from the hell storm inside. She wants impossible things and won't listen to reason, ever."

If anything, Charlie's mother is enabling her behavior. *Poor Charlie, she's having so much trouble, Eileen. You have to understand her.* If that was my mom, she'd be grounding her right now.

Jossie looks her over and then smirks. "I like you, honest."

She looks between Eileen and me with this weird fucking grin. "Come along. We've got a lot to do and barely any time to do it."

Jossie enters the boutique and Charlie McBean's insanity just like she does everything—a classy general ready to destroy the battlefield. We follow closely behind her.

"Watch the master in action," I whisper to Eileen.

"Vanessa, take five," Jossie tells the consultant. "Tell Antoine I'm here and I want a rack hand selected by him in front of me in the next ten minutes."

I think the consultant whimpers before running away. Jossie then turns on her old wedding planner charm.

"Well, hello there," Jossie says to Charlie who's glaring at yet another dress. "You must be, Charlotte. Jason has told me so much about you."

Charlie growls. "Who are you?"

"Oh, did Jason not inform you?" She says pleasantly then glares at me. "My apologies, darling. I'm Josslyn Udayar, professional wedding planner. I've successfully executed over a thousand weddings in the last decade, including some very high-profile weddings for clientele I can't name per our Non-Disclosure Agreements. You understand how it is, don't you, Charlotte?"

Charlie nods with this deer-in-the-headlights expression. "Yes, of course. Thank you so much for coming."

Jossie nods. "Jason, hand Ms. McBean her drink."

I fucking hurry to hand Charlie her weird ass drink. There's nothing I'm more terrified of than ruining Jossie's angle before she has a chance to work her magic.

"This was made especially for you," Jossie explains to her.

Charlie lifts her chin as if she had been crowned as the queen of the world. God have mercy on us all.

"Jason has informed me of your upset stomach," Jossie continues without missing a beat. "And we'll do everything to accommodate you."

Charlie blushes, but doesn't start shouting. Thank fuck.

"Now tell me, darling," Jossie says while squeezing Charlie's shoulder. "What is your dream dress?"

Charlie lights up, babbling nonsense about seams and mermaid tails? Something about tulips—I don't know, weddings have gotten more complicated in the last eight years.

Jossie nods thoughtfully. Thank fuck for her, I can't stand listening to Charlie anymore.

"Now what's our budget?" Jossie says pointedly.

Eileen says, "a thousand," at the same time Charlie says, "ten thousand."

They glare at each other.

"Why don't we ask the mother of the bride?" Jossie suggests.

Mrs. McBean shrugs looking at Eileen and then at me.

"Whatever Jason agrees to," Eileen concedes. "This is coming from his contribution."

All their gazes turn toward me. Great, thanks for throwing me under the bus. In the most surprising moment of the day, it's Charlie who gives me puppy dog eyes while Eileen stares me down threateningly.

Charlie's wrath I can live with. Eileen's, however, I don't want to find out what that looks like.

"Twenty-five hundred before tax," I compromise. "That's as high as I'll go."

Charlie starts to protest "But what about—"

"That'll do," Jossie says, patting Charlie on the back as she pushes her to the next room. "Now let's go see what Antoine's found for you, darling."

When Charlie's out of view, Mrs. McBean goes off on me. "You hired a wedding planner? Why couldn't you have done that last week?!"

I wince. I guess screaming runs in the family.

"Josslyn's retired," I point out. "She wouldn't take on the entire wedding but agreed out of the kindness of her, excuse my language, good fucking heart to help us out of this nightmare."

Mrs. McBean says, "She doesn't look a day over thirty," at the same time Eileen says, "Your assistant was a wedding planner?"

"Talking over each other must also run in the family," I think out loud. "But, yes and yes? One, she's thirty-five. Two, she *was* a wedding planner and *is* the most competent human being in existence. My career took off. I needed someone to manage my life for me. I made her an offer she couldn't refuse."

Mrs. McBean sags. "Well, thank you. For everything."

I try to take her halfhearted praise as an accomplishment but—

fuck. She's terrible at thanking people. It sounds so hollow and unsatisfying coming from her.

Is this what Eileen deals with all the time?

No wonder she's desperate for genuine approval.

When I look at Eileen though, there's that grateful smile of hers brightening the entire room. She makes me believe that it's worth the trouble.

But is it really worth it?

20

Eileen

THE CALL COMES in at a quarter to ten. Jason and I are in the middle of finishing the seating chart for the reception when my phone rings. Well, I'm arranging it while he's playing Game of Thrones with the red and blue flags. It's an epic battle, and if we're lucky, we'll have a red wedding.

This man is a closeted geek.

Lucky me, I have to deal with the wedding from hell and his nonsense.

When I check the caller ID, my smile flattens. It's my dad, who never calls for anything. My blood runs cold as I pick up the phone.

"Hey—"

"Your sister's been hospitalized," he says.

I don't pay much attention at the rest of the conversation. Just this vague idea that I repeat what he says to Jason, who takes the phone from me.

"Yes, sir," Jason says. "Littleton Adventist, I got it."

"We have to go," he tells me, moving the hair away from my face. "She's going to be okay."

I'm not sure how I get out of the house. I even wear shoes, who knows how I put them on—or when. There's a lot of white noise. I'm sure Jason speaks to me, but I can't think straight. My stomach is turning upside down.

Your sister is in the hospital is all I hear running through my head. It's just like the time she was in a bus accident back in sixth grade. Nobody could tell us where she was and if she was okay. I remember my mother's screams and my father crying.

"Everything will be fine," Jason whispers, squeezing my hand as we get into his car.

The street lamps flicker as we pass them driving through town. It's a dream, I try to rationalize to myself. Charlie's irresponsible but not reckless. Nothing could have happened to her.

Unless some freak accident happened.

The music playing in Jason's car is low enough that I can ignore it but loud enough that I don't have to exist in silence. I think some Tears for Fears plays at one point. How appropriate.

I shudder when he nudges me.

"I got you," he says quietly, opening the car door. "Just take my hand, okay?"

I trail behind him through the hospital. It's a blur of bright fluorescent lights and the disgustingly strong scent of antiseptic. He squeezes my hand every so often. Somehow, that reminds me to breathe.

In hindsight, I think he told me to do that—breathe whenever he squeezed.

We find her at some point, curled up in a hospital bed. She has an IV in her. She looks so gaunt with those bags under her eyes. I can't tell if they're from crying or lack of sleep. Maybe both.

My dad says some things. The doctor says some other things.

My mom glares at me. I must be crying or something. I don't know. She looks upset at me. But what did I even do? Fucking nothing.

Jason squeezes my hand. "It's fine, just breathe," he repeats in a low voice that only I can hear.

"We just need to keep her for observation," the doctor continues. "but we're strongly suggesting she stay on bedrest for the next few days."

"So she's okay? For the most part at least?" Jason asks. "And the baby?"

"Just your standard dehydration," the doctor explains. "But as I pointed out, she is a bit anemic which likely complicated things. The baby is fine, but she has to change her diet. We'll have to keep an eye on that."

My shoulders relax, and I finally let myself breathe deeply.

"How are you feeling, sweetheart?" Mom asks Charlie.

Charlie shrugs listlessly. "My wedding's ruined."

What? What is she even saying? Is that really what she's worried about right now?

"She's fucking kidding, right?" Jason mutters. "Un-fucking-believable."

Maybe she is doing that Charlie-thing where she projects what she's really scared of onto something more trivial.

I've never seen her look so sick and miserable before. This is terrible.

My mom glares at me again. Oh, maybe she was waiting for me to fix this.

I go to Charlie's bedside. She's always been taller than me. But right now, it feels like I'm towering over her. It makes my skin crawl.

My hand rubs her arm gently.

"Don't worry, this wedding is going to go off without a hitch," I say reassuringly.

"Eileen, it's hopeless," she whispers. "I can't put together a wedding in this condition."

I ignore the impulse to remind her—newsflash, you're not planning this wedding anyway. Jason sighs behind me. I know he's thinking the same thing.

But this isn't the time for a reality check. This is my sister and she needs me.

Instead, I hug her carefully. "We'll take care of everything, okay? I promise this'll be the wedding of your dreams. Just relax."

She hugs me back tightly, sobbing into my shoulder. It reminds me of when we were kids and I could rely on her. When all I had in the world was a sister who would kill for me, and that was plenty.

This is a no brainer. I'll do anything to make my sister happy.

———

"Let's take you home," Jason says around two in the morning.

I look up at him and smile. "You're still here."

He hands me a Styrofoam cup. "Who else would be handing you an endless supply of caffeine?"

I take a sip of the cup and glare at him. "This is tea."

"It's late," he informs me. "I'm cutting you off and driving you home."

"Mom and Dad left her."

"Marek is with her," he reminds me while he's looking toward Charlie's hospital room. "Only one person can stay. Let's go home."

"Do you think she's going to be okay?"

He gives me a patient look before sighing. "As long as she follows the doctor's instructions. Who diets while pregnant? Your sister has a lot to learn and too little time before she has to become a responsible mother."

I nod. The doctor gave her a lecture once she told him what she's been eating—or not eating—so her dress would fit.

"Let me take care of you for a change," he offers and extends his hand. "For once, let someone else worry about the weight of the world. Take a leap of faith and begin by believing that you can change the way you live your life."

But then what's there when my family can't depend on me?

21

Eileen

Eight days until the wedding

THE FOURTH PRIEST we've seen today walks us out of his office, shakes our hands warmly, and tells us, "I wish you luck on this journey."

This wild goose chase is growing desperate and nearly impossible. No one wants to officiate the last-minute wedding of a couple with a baby on the way. If by some miracle they agree to it, they get put off when they hear the bride and groom don't have time to meet with them.

They think it's weird when Jason goes to meet with them by himself, and they think it's sad—pitiful, I guess—when I go. In conclusion, our divide and conquer strategy didn't work one bit.

Our joint adventure hasn't proven to be more successful, however.

"At least he had the decency to be nice about saying no," I offer to Jason. "This one didn't lecture us about not having sex right as we enter his office.

He snorts as we walk briskly through the church. When we finally get in the car he sighs, gripping the steering wheel tightly.

"Sure, that guy was nice, but his 'house of God' was creepy as shit," he says.

I cross my arms, smirking. "You know, for a guy who isn't religious, you're pretty scared of churches—"

"They have dead people buried underneath them, and parts of dead people in glass displays, and sometimes the dead people are built into the walls!" he exclaims frantically. "How is that not terrifying?"

"This is a new church; I doubt there are people buried underneath," I correct him. "You watch way too many movies and documentaries."

"Still, churches are imposing, and they scare the fuck out of children," he says as he turns on the engine.

"Point taken," I concede.

We drive in silence for a while. Our next destination is an hour north of the city at this tiny little chapel. Huey Lewis and the News keep us company. Today's one of those rare overcast days that's whispering snow is coming.

Perfect. The last thing I need is Charlie fretting over her wedding getting ruined by the May weather. Mom already had to take a few days off from work so she'd calm down. And as if I had called her, she suddenly texts me.

Mom: *Did you find a priest?*

"Does it matter if this minister's Catholic?" Jason asks when we're a few miles away from our destination.

I groan and look at my phone.

Eileen: *We're on it.*

"Not really," I admit because at this point anyone would do it. "As long as they're religious and not too eccentric. I personally don't care."

Jason nods as he puts on his turn signal.

I continue, mostly to fill the silence. "It's for my grandparents' sake more than anyone. They'll get over the shotgun wedding as long as it's *legitimate*."

"Because being legally married by a legal minister is fake?" He burst into laughter.

What's with this guy and not taking anything serious?

"In their eyes, yeah," I admit.

He doesn't say anything. I think that's for the best. Regardless of how I feel, I know what my family is like.

"What if we make up a story?" I suggest, as Jason parks in front of the chapel.

He glances at me and arches his eyebrow. "Like what?"

"Like he just came back from the Peace Corps or she's gotten a job overseas—"

"Or they're both dying of cancer," he proposes.

"What the fuck? That's crazy." I glare at him.

"Newsflash, Eileen. That's exactly what you sound like—crazy," he gives me a little reality check.

I groan. "You're not taking this seriously."

He rolls his eyes. "Oh, I'm sorry. I didn't realize lying to a minister to get them to officiate this shit show of a wedding—"

"If it's such a shit show, what are you doing here? Why are you still help—"

"Because you've seen those idio—"

"Don't you dare call my sister an idiot," I shout.

Jason sags. He takes a deep breath and crosses his arms.

"Okay, I'm sorry," he says. Getting out of the car he speaks again as he opens the passenger door, "That was...maybe uncalled for. But what is this, Eileen? You're killing yourself over finding the right minister to make your *grandparents* happy."

I open my mouth to talk, but he lifts his index finger. "If it's not your sister, then it's your parents. Now we're up to your grandparents. When does the people pleasing end?"

I clench my jaw, trying to breathe.

"Does it ever end?" he asks quietly.

My eyes feel so hot and wet and uncomfortable. He doesn't get it, but how could he? Even I know this is too much.

"You saw how she was," I say finally. "How miserable she looked in that hospital bed. She needs help—"

"Hey, of course I did," he says as he loops his strong arms around my body. And suddenly, I feel safe.

I feel like I can breathe again and I'm strong enough to continue with this chaotic wedding.

"And she does need help," he mumbles not letting me go. "Weddings fucking suck to plan. All pregnancy complications not included."

His hug feels familiar. He must've done it back at the hospital.

It feels so strong, yet soft. I could bury my head in his chest and never leave. He smells like sandalwood and pine. Not the cheap body spray kind either, just like he's made out of timber and the mist of a forest.

I guess that makes sense. He's pretty magical as it is.

"But she needs a lot more help than getting this wedding planned," he says. "It'd help her a shit ton if you were more honest with her about how many hoops you're jumping through to get this done. Maybe she'd back off or even, I don't know, pitch in a little?"

I shake my head. "That's never going to happen."

"Which part?"

"All of it," I say.

He shrugs, trying to play it casual as he lets go of me. I know he's disappointed, though. It's okay, I think I'm a little disappointed in me too.

"Come on, Eileen," he says. "Let's see if this next one's willing to work with us."

"WELL, MY SCHEDULE IS OPEN FOR THE TWENTY-SEVENTH, fortunately," the third minister we've visited in the past couple of hours says after hearing the dates and logistics of the wedding.

"That's great news," I say, letting out a breath I must have been holding since yesterday.

"And I'm sure if your sister and her fiancé are every bit as well matched as you two," he pauses looking at our linked hands. "They'll have a very long and fortuitous marriage."

My brain grinds to a halt. He thinks Jason and I are together? Why would he say that? Shit, what do I say to that?

"Thanks, your holiness," Jason says as he releases my hand and wraps an arm around my shoulder. "We're not exactly there yet, but we appreciate the vote of confidence."

The minister smiles serenely. "I do have one observation that I think is important to address."

I swallow thickly. Shit, this is it, another rejection. "Yes?"

"This wedding is a week away," he says. "Did something happen to your last officiant or is there a special circumstance I should be aware of?"

I open my mouth to give whatever lame excuse my mind can muster up when Jason opens his *big mouth*.

"The answer's quite simple, your godliness," he says. "They're just two crazy kids madly in love with each other. I'm sure you understand this, being a man of God yourself, but their love goes deeper than the superficial junk everyone's into these days."

Great, he's going to start cursing and fuck our chances with this minister. Are we going to have to drive to New Mexico and kidnap some minister?

"Love isn't about the big, swooping gestures," Jason says. "It's about waking up just a little bit earlier to get coffee while they watch the news together. It's about trading off on the chores and responsibilities they hate and rewarding each other with smiles. It's about the conversations, compromises, and adventures that make their lives worth living. Love is about finding someone who wants to go on that crazy journey of life together so you can support each other every step of the way. And once you've found who you want to go on that journey with, it seems wrong to waste another moment apart."

My jaw drops.

Who is this man and what happened to Jason Spearman?

I had no idea he had something like this in him. I'm blown away. My head exploded, and so did my ovaries. Wow, that was one big speech, and I'll remember it for my entire life.

Who knew this guy felt anything or even thought that much about love? I've never seen him look so serious, or somber, before.

The minister seems to be just as pleased. He nods, offers us both handshakes and says, "Then I can't wait to officiate for such a thoughtful couple."

He confirms a few more details, reminds us to have the marriage certificate ready for the ceremony, and wishes us a good day.

When we get out of the chapel, I have to ask. "Where did that come from?"

"What?" Jason gives me a side glance before opening the passenger door. He waits until I am seated to close the door and walk around to the driver's side.

He gets in the car, turns on the engine and before pulling out he says, "The lovey-dovey crap?"

"Uh, yes," I confirm, waiting anxiously for his answer. "Where'd you learn to wax poetic like that?"

He shrugs, refusing to look me in the eye as we head back toward Denver. The silence is so fucking uncomfortable on the way back.

It's not our normal, companionable silence. He wants to say something; I fucking know he does. Every so often he'll look over in my direction, mouth opening hesitantly before snapping shut... again, and again, and *again*.

Finally, he says something, "I didn't come up with that on the fly, okay?"

"So, you just had a romantic speech prepared," I say. "I carry hand sanitizer wipes; you carry your own lectures for all occasions."

He shrugs and mutters, "They were part of my wedding vows."

I sit up straight. Jason doesn't wear a ring. He's never mentioned a wife or a girlfriend. He sure as fuck acts like the kind of guy who would never get married.

So what's the fucking deal here?

I say as much out loud.

"I had a wedding, once," he says stiffly. "Didn't get married, have never been married."

Without thinking, I squeeze his shoulder. "Wanna talk about it?"

Jason shakes his head, laughing shakily.

He starts talking anyway.

22

Jason

Ten Years Ago

AS THE BLACK EYE PEAS blare on the speakers with their usual nonsense lyrics, I walk toward Greta, my beautiful girlfriend, who seems to be having a blast tonight.

"You know I have to admit," she says. "This party is pretty great."

Okay, I know most guys hype up their partners, but fuck. I have the best girlfriend in the world.

She spelunks in her free time. She runs the social media for the local dog rescue because she had extra time in her schedule. Plus, she's smart as shit, graduating top of her class with a degree in poli-sci. She knows how to handle social situations the way my older brother wishes I could.

"Oh, if you have to," I say jokingly, "Then I guess I should've ordered those flying unicorns after all."

She laughs, swatting my arm playfully. "Stop, I just mean this is nice..."

"But?"

"A little much for a graduation party, don't you think?" she contemplates the house.

I look around. Maybe the chocolate fountain is overkill, but she deserves the best. Champagne, her favorite food from the Italian Bistro down the street, and a frozen yogurt machine to give her unlimited supply of tart flavored ice cream with her favorite toppings.

"Well, I was hoping you wouldn't mind if I double dip a little," I add with a smile as the pocket of my jeans burns with her next surprise. "I want to make this a combo party."

"Oh?" she says with that crooked smile I love so much. Fuck, I could look at it forever.

She takes a sip of her champagne and rolls her eyes. "What else are we celebrating tonight?"

This is it. Don't fuck it up, Jason.

"Why don't you turn around and find out?" I say.

Greta turns around just as Jack and Alex pull the chord on a banner that reads "Will you marry me?" I get down on one knee as she reads it, holding the three-carat princess cut I bought for her last month.

Greta turns around slowly. "Uh, is this—" She gasps.

"Babe," I say, licking my lips. "All my life I've wanted someone who gets me as much as you do. And now that you're done with school, I never want to be away from you again. So, what do you say? Would you make me the luckiest man on Earth and be my wife?"

Her lip trembles a bit. Tears well up in her eyes as she nods enthusiastically. I must also be crying because the next thing I know, she is tackling me in a hug and everything is blurry around me.

She said yes.

I mean I *knew* she would say yes. But holy fuck this is real. I get to spend the rest of my life with the love of my life. This is the happiest fucking day of my entire life.

Jack was wrong. He claimed we're too young for this shit. I'm only twenty-five and settling down too soon.

What does he know about being ready?

The party kicks back into high gear. Family members keep stopping by to say congratulations. Greta shows off her ring whenever someone asks to see it, but that's it. I expected her to be shoving it in everyone's face.

She'll gloat about anything she can justify. This seems like a pretty easy thing to gloat about. I knew mixing parties was a terrible idea. Is that it?

Huh, maybe she didn't like the ring. I knew I should've taken my sisters with me, instead of Jack and Alex. They know more about what women like.

"If you want to change it, we can check other jewelers," I suggest, hugging her by the waist.

"Are you kidding?" she asks. "It's wonderful, just like you."

I look into her beautiful blue eyes, and as I'm bending over to kiss her I hear June calling my name, "Jason, where are you? It's time to start this party!"

My sisters start up karaoke. Of course I get swept up in that and a few impromptu covers of Springsteen and REO Speedwagon. I realize after a few turns with family members that I haven't seen Greta in a while. I let Marek take the next one by himself.

"Wait, where are you going?" he says, panicked.

"Gotta find my fiancée, bro," I inform. "Can't do a duet of Benny and the Jets without her."

More people must have arrived after the proposal. It's so fucking packed in here. I wade through this huge crowd, but still nothing.

"Have you seen Greta?" I ask Jackson who is by the door with Vivian, his girlfriend. She looks a little annoyed as I approach them.

"No man, maybe you went a little overboard."

Vivian huffs. "At least she got a three-carat ring."

I pat Jack on the shoulder and continue my way around. *Good luck with that one, buddy.*

"Maybe she's in the bathroom," I murmur to myself as I head in that direction.

She's nowhere to be found in the hallway bathroom, but I hear something coming from my bedroom. Greta's sitting on the floor next to the window, sobbing. I run to her side, clutching her tightly.

"Hey," I shush her gently. "What's going on?"

Greta shakes her head, burying it in my shoulder. She sobs even harder. I take a deep breath, hugging her tighter. Eventually, the sobs die out.

"I'm sorry," she says quietly.

"Sorry for what?"

She pulls away, shrugging. Her eyes won't meet mine. It's unnerving.

"I'm just so overcome with emotions, Jason," she says. "I knew we were heading in this direction, but—"

"Hey no, don't be sorry for that." I clear her tears with my thumb.

Seeing her this sad is breaking me down.

"If it's too soon we can slow things down," I offer. "Or just have a really long engagement."

She shakes her head. "No, nope, you've waited so long for this. I can't stall your dreams any longer."

"Greta, babe, you are my dream," I remind her. "Nothing's going to change that, alright?"

Greta finally looks up at me. Her eyes are still so fucking watery. I kiss the corner of her left eye.

"Okay," she whispers. "Let's do it. Let's get married."

In hindsight, I don't know who she was trying to convince—herself or me.

23

Jason

Nine Years Ago

A YEAR INTO BEING ENGAGED, our wedding planning is in high gear. There's less than six months until our big day, and there's so much that still needs to be done.

The wedding planner keeps calling my cellphone asking for Greta. Usually, it's while I'm at work. It keeps getting my boss aggravated but, it's fine. I won't be here long anyway. Once we save up enough and Greta passes the bar in New York, we're starting a brand new life.

My apps are selling like hot candy, and maybe I can make a living off of them.

"Uh, why don't you call her cellphone?" I say at least once a week.

"She's not picking up, again," she normally says, but this time—

"I don't care anymore. You're available, she's not," she comes to that conclusion and I'm fucked. "Will you just tell me if *you* prefer blue hydrangeas or blue roses?"

"Uh," I say not knowing what a fucking hydrangea is, "Hydrangeas?"

It sounds fancier, right. Greta likes different. There's nothing more different than a flower you can't pronounce.

"Perfect," she speaks loudly, then mumbles something I can't make out before coming back to the line. "Tell your bride if she ghosts me again, I'll be charging extra. Is that clear?"

"Crystal," I say.

"It's Josslyn," she corrects jokingly.

"Can I call you Jossie?"

"Only my friends call me that," she announces.

Damn, she flips back to professional in nothing flat. That's not only the impressive thing about her business acumen.

"Noted," I say. "Hey if you ever want to get out of the wedding planning game—"

"You're not the first man to offer me a business proposition." She stops me right in my tracks. Damn, she's not an easy person to convince. Or maybe she's the perfect one to have in your corner. "So, I'll tell you what I told the others. I make six figures. Unless you're willing to match that plus unbelievable benefits, stop while you're ahead."

"Hear you loud and clear," I respond.

———

"She has you picking wedding colors?" Alex says with an amused face.

We met at our favorite sports bar to watch the Sharks play the Canucks. So far, it's a bust. We're getting slammed by the Canadians. It's only the first period and they already scored two goals.

"Whoosh," says Jack, pretending to handle a whip. "Aren't we a little whipped?"

"What do you want me to do? She went back to school," I remind him. "*Law school.*"

Alex smirks and adds. "He likes his women pretty and smart. She's so intelligent, she's already regretting being with this asshole."

"Shut up, fucker!"

"Aw, Jase didn't like my joke?" He takes the pitcher and heads to the bar.

"Is everything okay?" Jack asks seriously.

"Why are you asking?"

"I don't know. Greta seemed a little strange last Sunday while you guys visited our parents." He shrugs. "If you need to talk..."

"Call June or Jeannette?" I ask, knowing his usual joke.

He smirks. "You got it, man."

We're fine, I repeat inside my head. It's the pressure of school, the wedding jitters, and her fear of not getting an internship for the summer.

———

LATER THAT WEEK, GRETA COMES HOME LATE WITH TAKEOUT. It's the first time I see her arriving. Every day she's been getting home around midnight or so she says. I am fast asleep on the couch when she makes her way to the bedroom.

"You looked so tired last night, I didn't have the heart to wake you up," she said the first night, and the second, and even earlier today while I was making the morning coffee.

We sit quietly across from each other in the living room. Some days she's really into using our little dining room table. "Playing adult" is what she calls it.

Greta always says we'll know we're adults when we become them. I don't know if that's true. I've been on my own since I turned twenty-one. She moved in with me two years later. And I don't fucking know what I'm doing any better than I did four years ago.

If anything, I think I have less control of my own life, and I can't see what my future looks like. Her absent mind makes everything more unexpected. But not in the exciting, surprisingly way. No, it leaves me feeling insecure and shaky.

A year ago, I was walking toward something solid. Now, I'm on top of a tightrope wondering if I'll make it across or if a tornado will push me and I'll fall down.

Alone.

"The wedding planner called me again," I say casually over sushi.

She groans. "What does she want now?"

"Wanted to know if we preferred hydrangeas or roses," I inform her.

"Roses, obviously," Greta says, rolling her eyes.

"Oh well." I cut myself off.

There's nothing I can add here unless she wants to get pissed off at me like that time I told the wedding planner I like vanilla cake. Apparently, *we* only want a chocolate wedding cake with raspberry cream filling.

My sisters, God bless their souls, offered to give me a hand with this—in exchange for compensation. I would love to take them up on it, but I know Greta would hate if she knows the twins are making any decisions in regard to her big day.

"Your sisters hate me," she keeps telling me every time I bring them up. "Sometimes, being around your family is a full-time job."

It's a balancing act, I understand. One day, we'll look at this period and laugh. If only we could fast forward time.

"It's fine," she says tiredly. "It doesn't matter anyway."

We fall into silence again. Shit's been tough for her, between law school and the wedding. We don't have much time to talk anymore and when we do, she's tired as fuck. It's really been putting a strain on our relationship.

Patience, Dad told me. Everything will work out the way it is meant to be. I can only hope he is right. That once the planning lets up a bit, she'll relax enough to let her guard down again.

I miss her quirky laugh. The way she used to indulge my weird love of 80s music or how she used to trust me to make everything better for her. I just want her to be happy.

"You know," I say hesitantly. "My schedule's a bit more consistent than yours."

She glances at me, her lips pressed together. My stomach drops. This might be a terrible idea and she's just going to dump my ass.

But what if that's the solution?

"Maybe I should help out more with the wedding," I suggest. "You know, call the shots a little more so you don't have to."

Her gaze narrows and she asks, "How would you know what I want?"

"We can make a list with the basics. I'll go from there."

Greta nods as she takes a long sip of wine. "That would be fantastic. You know I can't keep up with Jacklyn's—"

"Josslyn," I correct her.

"Whatever," she says waving her hand. "She's too much and she has to have a contingency for everything. Who needs that in their life?"

Us, I think, but don't say out loud.

"So it's settled," I conclude invigorated by this new plan. "I'll take the helm of the SS Spearman Wedding."

Greta reaches over the coffee table to squeeze my hand. Her mouth smiles, but it never reaches her eyes.

That's been happening a lot more lately.

But any time I try to bring it up she gets more upset or pushes me away. One time I asked her if there's more she needed from me. She left and didn't come back for three days.

I've stopped trying to ask. For now, at least.

Once things settle down, shit will get back to normal, I try to argue to myself. *We'll* get back to normal. It's just a few more months of tight schedules and tensions. After that we can take our honey-moon, cool off.

If she isn't happy then, we'll work through it. Whatever it takes to get her smiling for real again.

"Thank you," she says. "I can't tell you how much this means to me."

I shrug, blushing slightly. "You can show me after the reception."

Of course, she never got the chance.

24

Jason

Eight Years Ago

WEDDING planning isn't for the faint of heart.

Save the dates, invites, flowers, caterer, RSVPs, seating charts, and so much more. If my business doesn't take off, I'm going to work for Josslyn. While working on this, I even created an application for wedding planners, another for brides, and even got a fun countdown for grooms.

We are ready for the big day. At least, I think everything is ready. I have changed my vows five times. They don't sound right. Something is missing. There's just so much I want Greta to know.

This day has to be perfect for her. It's the most important day of our lives. We're finally here.

Are there enough words to express what she means to me?

I just need her to feel the way she did before... I can't remember when was the last time that she smiled without worries. Fuck, the last time she smiled *period*. A real smile. One that showed in her eyes, not just a movement of her lips.

When I finish putting on my tux, I decide to write another set of vows. Sixth time is the charm, right? Once I finish them, I begin to rehearse them. I think this time I got them just right.

"I want you to know that I didn't think I was the kind of person who could fall in love, but now that I have you, I can't imagine life any other way. Love isn't about the big, swooping gestures. It's about waking up just a little bit earlier to get coffee while we watch the news together. It's about trading off on the chores and responsibilities we hate and rewarding each other with smiles. Love is about finding someone who wants to go on that crazy journey of life together so you can support each other every step of the way. And I'm so happy I got—"

Jack won't stop tapping my fucking shoulder.

I groan. "What part of *let me rehearse my vows,* is so fucking unclear, dude?"

"It's almost time," he says. "Josslyn came to check on you."

Taking a deep breath, I lift my gaze from the paper. We've been standing just out of view from the guests for an hour now, behind some rose hedges. The botanical gardens look beautiful today.

Everything's so lush and green after the first rain of spring— which was last night and not this morning, thank fuck.

A couple hundred of our closest friends, family, and Jack's business contacts who *absolutely* had to be here, are all just beyond the hedges waiting for this shindig to start.

"She's late," Jack informs me. "Shouldn't we do something?"

The guests aren't the only people waiting for this to start.

"Like what?' I crook an eyebrow. We can't start without her. "She's still getting ready, so what?"

"It's been a while, Jason," he says.

Greta's limo was supposed to arrive two hours ago. She still isn't here. I scrub my face. The notecards I'm holding scratch me up a little, but I'm beyond fucks to give. But what if something happened to her?

"Where is the bridal party?"

"They are in the bridal sweet," Jason informs me.

My back tenses. What if something really happened to her?

A car accident. Maybe she went to sleep last night and never woke up. I run through all the scenarios that would keep her away from us, but everything is just stupid.

We texted each other earlier. I look at my phone again. There they are, our last messages.

Jason: I can't wait to spend to spend the rest of our lives together.

Jason: Today is the day we begin our future.

Greta: It's a good day to start again.

She's just as excited as I am. Nothing happened to her. She's not here because... I check the time. It's ten thirty. The ceremony doesn't start until eleven. What if she decided to get ready at home?

Greta does everything at her own accord.

"Dude, just—wait like a goddamn adult," I finally snap.

Jack furrows his brow, then shrugs. "So, you're not worried?"

"Of course, I am," I whisper. "But it's our wedding day. She can have some time if she needs it. This is a big fucking deal."

———

I COULDN'T WAIT FOR THE DAY TO CALL HER MY WIFE, BUT I would wait a million years if I could finally call her mine. Except you can't force anyone to be yours.

My heart lurches when it's thirty past noon and Josslyn approaches me to say, "They have to get the place ready for the next ceremony."

"What if she comes?"

She hands me an envelope, "The limo just arrived. The driver had this for you."

The pain lassos my chest, yanking it tighter. I'm unable to breathe. All I've done since the moment I met this woman is love her.

What else did she need from me? Under the gazebo decorated with blue flowers, I drop to the floor defeated.

I prepared for everything, except this.

She's not coming. I never knew hurt until my heart broke into a million pieces. My insides were being excavated, prowled, and removed from within as the minutes passed. Mom whispers a few words. Dad seconds them with some others.

Jack squats, patting my shoulder and mumbling more nonsense.

I shake my head. Mom and Dad walk away after they assure me that everything will be fine. They are here to support me. As if it's that easy. We had plans, a future.

"Do you want me to call off the wedding?" Jack announces.

I snort showing him the envelope. "Sorry, dude. I think she called dibs on that part."

Taking a deep breath, I find a smidge of strength. I get up in front of a few hundred people who are all staring at me with pitying frowns.

"Thank you for taking some time in your lives to share this day with us." I use part of the speech I planned on saying during the reception.

"Unfortunately, there's a change of plans. But don't go just yet. There's a ballroom with our name and lots of food waiting for you guys. It's already been paid for, and we want to thank you for making it out here so, please enjoy," I say with the most normal sounding voice I can fucking muster.

Since instead of presents, we asked for them to donate to the animal shelter where Greta worked, we won't be able to return any of the *gifts*. But at least they get a sweet write off during tax season.

A couple of hours later, I head to the ballroom. Everyone seems to have fun at the reception. It's still gorgeous. Greta's family comes up to apologize at one point, but I wave them off. It's not like they knew.

Even if they had, they couldn't have stopped her. Neither would I have wanted them to.

The longer the night trudges on, the more everything falls into place in my fucking head. How evasive she was about planning the wedding and the honeymoon. How aggravated she got the closer we got to the wedding.

For fuck's sake, I chide myself. Crying at the engagement party, and at random points in the middle of the night every so often thereafter. Those were the signs.

That fucking text. She was starting her new life, today. I wasn't part of the plan.

But why wasn't she honest from the beginning? I tried talking to her about it. Confronting her. At some point I got so fucking tired of being pushed away and told "everything is fine."

What else could I do but believe her? I begged and I pleaded.

She didn't want to get married. Message finally received.

I wonder if she ever wanted to get married. If the problem was us getting married or if our ship had sailed but no one had bothered to send me the memo. I guess that's what I get for proposing in front of all her family.

Fuck, I'm a dick.

Sometime later, Josslyn pulls me into a secluded hallway behind the kitchen of the reception venue.

"I tracked her down," she says.

"How?"

"I have my ways," she says neutrally. "She just landed in JFK. She had a one-way ticket to New York."

One way. "She's not coming back."

Ever, goes unsaid.

"I bet she got that internship she mentioned at the beginning of this school year," I say out loud. All the pieces are coming together. "We could've gone together.

"What a fucking moron," I exclaim, this time with anger.

"Was she ever going to show up?" I think out loud. "At least she could've had the guts to tell me to my face that I wasn't part of her future."

I pull out the envelope she'd given me earlier. It has my name scrawled in Greta's chicken-scratch handwriting.

Jason,

You're a great guy.

I snort at how she started the fucking letter. Really? You're a great guy? She's studying fucking law. I expected something fancier and more legitimate from her.

I'm just a fucking good guy. The most stupid asshole in the history of human kind.

Please forgive me. I'm not very good at this sort of thing. But please know that right now, my heart is breaking for us. We were good together. I remember that we were happy, but I'm a firm believer that happiness can only hold you together for so long.

As the days passed, our time together became stifling. My plans on going to New York were stopped by your eagerness to do it just right. This isn't about you, Jason. It's about me and what I want for my future.

I can't do this.

I can't be your wife.

There's so much more for me than staying with you for the rest of my life. I know what you want, a house like your parents with just as many children, but what about me?

I've worked hard to have a career. This is my time. I have to grow and reach for my dreams. Every person has her own destiny, and mine isn't here.

Not with you.

Not with a husband, a minivan, and a bunch of children.

I hope one day you understand me. Thanks for your years of kindness and support.

All my love,

Greta

I TAKE A SHUDDERING BREATH. "FUCK."

This hallway is too fucking narrow and hot. My suit is like a boa constrictor. Something gets caught in my throat. I keep reading this one line over and over and again.

Every person has her own destiny, and mine isn't here.
Not with you.

Had any of this mattered to her? Did any of this matter?

Did she ever love me?

"Jason, listen to me," Josslyn says somewhere above me. "Take a deep breath and hold it for five seconds."

I follow her instruction, or try to at least. She puts a hand on the back of my shoulder and rubs circles into it. Breathing gets a little easier.

"You're going to be alright," she says. "It hurts now, but in the long run—"

"She saved us both a lot of pain later on," I say numbly. "Yeah, that's good."

"And because you're a good man who cares very deeply about things," she continues.

But I wave my hand to stop her. "I think I'm just a jackass," I conclude. "Who bulldozed his way into a wedding no one wanted? I pushed her too far."

Josslyn clears her throat. "You can't know that without talking to her. However, I've seen thousands of couples get married, and at the risk of sounding unprofessional, this is only the second time I've seen a fiancé so invested in their partner's happiness and fulfillment as you."

I snort.

"No, I'm serious," she insists. "There's a difference between being misguided but well intentioned and being a, quote, *jackass.*"

She squeezes my shoulder. "Listen to me. You're not a jackass, Jason Spearman."

I nod, not really caring if she's just bullshitting me right now. I wouldn't blame her if she was. I'm a fucking mess and I still need to give her the last ten percent of her pay.

"If you ask Jack for the last check, he'll give it to you and bill me later," I say, not taking my eyes off the brick wall across from me. "You know, in case you wanted to get out of here already."

Surprisingly, she squeezes my hand. "You're not very good at having friends, are you?"

"Are we friends?"

"Can you afford to hire me?"

I laugh, lean on the wall, and lower myself until I'm sitting down. "No, you're like... three years out of my budget."

Josslyn sits down next to me. "Then I guess you'll have to settle for friendship."

"Okay," I say, putting my head on her shoulder.

She wraps an arm around my shoulder and honestly? It's nice. There's something wet in my eyes that's probably sweat. I didn't know how much I needed a hug right about now until this *friend* offered me one.

"Hey, Jossie?" I say eventually.

"Yes, dear," she says.

"What the fuck do I do now?"

She shrugs.

Yeah, that sounds about right. But I make a vow, because that's why I busted my ass for the past year. To make a commitment. If not to Greta, at least to myself.

I won't allow anyone to hold me down again. No matter what, I'll look after myself and never get attached because I arrived into this world alone and that's exactly how I'll leave it.

25

Jason

5 Days until the Wedding

NOTHING SAYS Armageddon like getting close to a wedding day.

Poor Eileen. She has no idea that between now and the big day, the entire world can end. The only reason I continue humoring her is because I swear to God, this woman needs someone to watch over her or she'll be trying to save the entire McBean clan.

"You know Jossie's going to have a conniption over this," I warn her as she puts money in a street meter.

Eileen stares at me incredulously. "Over getting Charlie's dress altered?"

I nod.

She smirks. "Jossie is cool. I don't get why you're as afraid of her as if she was the big bad wolf and you were one of the three little piggies."

She laughs at her own joke, and after several seconds and a few confused glares from the people passing by, she takes a breath and says, "Why would you say that, little piggy?"

I lift my chin, feigning anger, but I can only stay like that for so long when her lips have that fantastic smile that just makes me breathe easier.

"It's just a few stitches, don't worry. She won't notice."

"She will, and she'll freak out over getting Charlie's dress altered way too fucking last minute by someone *Jossie* doesn't know," I say pressing my lips together and giving her a disapproving look. "Or approves of for that matter."

Eileen grunts. "I told you, Seamus—"

"—*Seamus*—"

"—is a family friend who can do it in no time," she explains. "He's the one who altered Charlie's baptismal gown to fit Sam and me too."

A baptismal gown?

"I can't believe you know a dude named Seamus," I say instead of asking about this famous baptismal gown. Let's hope Marek's kid doesn't have to wear it too. "That's so funny, I don't even need to make a joke for it."

"Good," she warns me.

As she opens the door to the shop for me, she gives me that gaze of *you better behave or else* and warns me, "If you make a joke in front of him, I'll kick you out of here myself."

"Fine, fine." I raise my hands as if surrendering, even though I'm carrying the freaking gown, but caution her, "If he shows up in a leprechaun outfit with a pot of gold, I can't be held responsible for my actions."

She laughs at that one. Score.

The shop isn't as asphyxiating as the bridal shop we were in a few days ago. In fact, I find it cozy. On one side, Seamus has his altering shop and on the other, he and his family have a tattoo parlor. How badass is that?

"Eileen," a guy who's about the same age as my father receives us. I stare at his tattoo sleeves and eye the chair.

"Tattoos are like marriages," the guy says.

I swallow, wondering what he means by that. I have a couple of tattoos on my back but none of them are related to Greta or what I feel for weddings and the fucking institution of marriage.

"How can those two relate?" Eileen asks curiously.

"They are meant to be forever. So, when you think you're ready for either one, you have to stop yourself and think about them thoroughly. Think about what you want, where you want it, and if you'll be able to live with it for the rest of your life. If you can't answer any of those questions, then stay away from the needle—or the commitment."

"Welp." Eileen turns to me and claps her hand. "This wedding isn't mine, and we're not here to get a tattoo. So, let's get to the point."

"Down the hall, my dear," Seamus indicates the way. "After you change, go onto the pedestal."

I follow her but wait outside.

"Okay, second point," I say while she's changing in the bathroom at this tailor's...shop? Store? Office? Convenient location with multiple businesses. "If this is *Charlie's* wedding dress why is *Eileen* getting fitted for it."

"Because *Charlie* wishes she had *Eileen's* boobs and will stuff her bra regardless," she explains. "So might as well give her the room to do that. Plus, she went to the doctor to make sure she's healthy enough for her honeymoon."

"Wait, honeymoon?" I don't remember approving the cost of a trip to Acapulco.

"My grandparents from Mom's side decided to gift her a honeymoon to The Keys," she explains. "It's not Acapulco like Marek wanted, but it's a beach."

"I knew they would find some sucker to pay for it," I mumble.

"What's that?" she shouts.

"Nothing," I say innocently. "You realize she's taller than you, right? And don't brides like, wear high heels?"

"Can I reference your tragic backstory?"

"As long as you admit it's tragic," I concede.

"It's extremely tragic," she says indulgently.

I'm satisfied with that. "Proceed."

"Well, not everyone wants to wear heels, pal," she says. "You can't supply what you know about one woman and apply it to every woman you meet after that."

Are we still talking about Charlie and her?

That's— "You're saying I'm a dick."

"I didn't say that!" she shouts through the bathroom door.

"You just quoted misogyny 101." I point emphatically. Damn, I wish she had x-ray vision to see through this door. "Don't assume all women are the same, that's like, elementary level shit."

"I guess," she says. "If you know it, then I don't understand why you still do it."

I run a hand through my hair. "And you're calling me out for it. Wow."

"Well, didn't you just assume every woman would wear heels to her wedding?" She protests.

I think about it for a second. "Shit, wow. Yeah, my bad. Thanks for calling me out on my bullshit. I'll keep that in mind next time I try to make a blanket statement."

"You're welcome?" she says hesitantly. "You don't need to thank me for anything."

I cross my arms. "Have you ever been apologized to or thanked by a dude? Or, you know, ever been apologized to or thanked in general, *ever*?"

Her family doesn't seem like the type to do either one period.

Eileen laughs. "Apologies, that's a good one."

"I'm being serious," I argue.

"I don't even have time to see dudes," she says with a grunt. "Let alone have a long enough conservation with one of them where they could mess up and then be convinced into apologizing."

The door creaks as she opens it. And wow, she's gorgeous. I'm breathless, stunned, and speechless. The strapless top fits her perfectly, showing off her delicate shoulders.

I want to run my mouth across her soft skin, feather kisses along her long neck. As she walks, the bottom just flows off like this ethereal, angelic cloud.

Fuck, she's breathtakingly beautiful. I could look at her forever.

"What do you think?" she says with a smile as she walks toward me. She beams as she twirls a couple of times. "How do I look?"

"Amazing," I say without thinking.

She frowns. "What?"

"Uh... amazingly tall," I say, producing a fake laugh. "How'd you get so tall?"

This is so awkward I feel like I'm drowning in quicksand.

She squints and shows her feet. "High heels. Remember?"

"Yeah, but..." Shit, think fast. What the fuck do I follow up with — "You're taller than Charlie normally is?"

"Oh," she says, shoulders sagging. "Charlie's wearing heels to the wedding."

"But you just said—"

"Don't assume every *woman* wants to wear high heels to her wedding," she says with a smirk. "I never said don't assume *Charlie* wouldn't wear high heels to her wedding."

I burst into genuine laughter. "I can't believe you."

Eileen giggles, hip checking me as she heads to where the tailor is waiting for her. I tilt my head, enjoying the view. So fucking beautiful.

My mind short circuits when the tailor asks her to lift her skirt. The heels make her toned legs look like a mile long. My eyes follow them up, up, and I wish I could undress her slowly.

I fan myself. It's too fucking hot and my pants are incredibly tight.

"I need to use the restroom," I shout before running toward the back of the store.

This can't be happening to me. I slam the bathroom door behind me, triple check that it's locked.

I slap myself. "Pull it together, dude," I chastise myself. "You're not jerking off in public just because you've got some sort of..."

What is it? A crush? Lust for this amazing, smart, and funny chick? Or it's just a wedding fetish?

Yeah, I think to myself. Wedding fetish. That has to be it. I never got to see my bride wearing her wedding dress, so it must be why I'm just thinking about ripping that dress off Eileen and tasting her. No other reason.

How do I get rid of it? Or her?

26

Jason

"ARE YOU SURE YOU'RE OKAY?" she asks holding my face with her soft hands. "You don't look sick."

"It's fine, just an upset stomach," I lie.

No way I'm going to explain to her that I had to talk myself out of a boner in a public bathroom, *like a teenager*.

"You sure?" She moves my face closer to hers, and I stop breathing as I feel her breath across my face, and she's so close to me, I can smell her sweet perfume.

God, why are you torturing me?

I can feel my pants shrinking in the groin area one more time. I have to go home. She should call an Uber. There's no way I can spend one more day with her.

"Would you mind if we go to an antique shop?" she asks. "It's just a few blocks from here."

"Antique shopping?" I frown.

"Yeah," she says, releasing my face and pulling her journal. "Charlie said she wants some 'rustic' decorations... which we probably can't afford, but if I get some reference photos, we can make a few things."

So, if it weren't weird enough that she knows a tailor named *Seamus*, she just happens to have a regular antique shop she frequents, owned by a woman named Maria.

"Ay, amor," Maria says. "What are you looking for today? Another watering can for your sculpture?"

Another watering can? And a sculpture?

"Not today, Maria," Eileen answers looking around. "I had to put that project on the back burner. But if you have any old copper wire—"

"Say no more," Maria exclaims. "I've been saving some for you. I'll have Reginald get it out of the back."

Okay, this brings up a lot of questions. Mainly what is the copper wire for? How often does Eileen come here? Who the fuck has a favorite antique shop? And when the fuck does she have time to breathe if she's been doing school and work and elaborate art projects for years?

And when was the last time she went on vacation? Or a date?

Then again, it's not really my place to ask. Talking about places, this isn't my place to be at—an antique shop with a woman.

Just as I'm thinking about how to get out of this place, I receive a text from Jack.

Jack: *We're back in Denver. Emmeline wants to know if you need any help?*

Thank you for nothing, I think.

Jason: *We got everything under control.*

Jack: *We?*

Jason: *Eileen, the sister of the bride, and me.*

Jack: *Em wants to know what you're doing at an antique shop?*

I look around, what the hell?

Jason: *I missed her so much, I had to go somewhere that reminds me how much I don't like her.*

Jason: *Seriously, how does she know?*
Jack: *Jossie told her. She's working at the office.*

I run a hand through my hair. These women are driving me fucking insane. After this wedding, I am leaving for some tropical island and I'm not coming back until I exorcize... Eileen comes to stand right next to me and shows me an old crate.

"We're here for that old thing?" I scrunch up my nose. "We can get them at Michaels."

"No, this is for me," she says. "Maria, do you have any more of these?"

"Maria," I sing under my breath. "I just met a girl named Maria."

Eileen hip-checks me. "Knock it off."

"Oh, *come on, Eileen*," I say. "Don't go lame on me. You're the only fun person in this crazy mixed-up world of ours."

She blushes. Shit, what did I—

Huh, maybe she thought I was flirting with her.

It's true, though. She's the only person I've ever met that's worth a damn, comedically at least. Which, granted, is probably far more important to me than the average guy.

We wander around the shop for a while. She stops every so often to take a picture, say a few things about some object she's found. I've been writing notes down in my phone for later.

"What I'm wondering," I say once we're further into the store. "Is if you're an artist—"

"*Was* an artist," she corrects.

"—How did you end up in physical therapy of all things? Isn't there, I don't know, art therapy or something?"

"That was the plan," she says, placing an old hat on top of my head and snapping a picture. "Or at least the back up to being a muralist. But you can't get a Master's in Art Therapy if you don't have a BFA in art."

"And your parents—fuck, that's shitty," I say.

"It was," she surprisingly agrees. "But physical therapy still does a lot of good. And sometimes I can get away with art related activities depending on the patient's needs and interests."

I nod impressed by her make lemonade out of all the lemons her family has been throwing her.

"Theatre doesn't have to be your career to make you happy, right?" she says suddenly.

"That was random." I rub the back of my neck. She's right though.

Eileen shrugs. "I was just thinking, you can act for fun. You don't have to give it up."

"It doesn't really matter," I say. "That's who I was, not who I am now."

"And you reciting lyrics from West Side Story is what exactly?" she says as she walks backwards through an aisle of lamps.

Fuck, she knows this place too well.

"I'm not totally heartless," I say.

"So you admit you're depriving yourself of your greatest joy in life," she says. "Singing, dancing, and acting on a stage."

"Words in my mouth much?"

She's so invested in this. Why? Why does it matter if I go after my childhood dream? Who cares?

Eileen stops walking. She looks at me intently.

"You deserve to be happy too, you know," she says softly.

Which— "I know," I say.

"Do you?"

"I am," I counteract.

"Are you?"

She says it so patiently and with this fucking kindness—what is her deal?

Eileen's out here plucking at my heartstrings, trying to get me to care about, what, exactly? My self-fulfillment? My happiness?

Who gave her any right to barge into my life like that?

"Why do you even care?" I say quietly.

The conversation fucking dies right then and there. Eventually she shrugs and we move on with our lives, but I still don't get it.

Why does she have to be so considerate and caring? Why does everything she does have to be delightfully odd? Why does she have to be so fucking smart and funny and perfect—

It hits me like a ton of bricks.

Fuck. She's perfect.

Eileen McBean is my fucking dream girl.

I guess I don't have a wedding fetish.

27

Jason

IT'S HER.

No fucking wedding dress fetish.

Eileen is flipping my world upside down. She makes me go against my better judgment. This is not the first time I tell myself to stay away from her and instead, what do I do?

I invite her over to my house.

Not only that, we brought Max along because the poor sweet cat has been neglected for the last couple of weeks. If Emmeline learns any of this, she's going to give me shit for the rest of my natural life.

And actually, I give zero fucks.

So here we are, spending our evening working on signage for the wedding.

They are rustic, classy, and made with love.

Technically speaking, Eileen works on designing, sketching, hand lettering, and painting signs for the wedding. She's the craftier of the two of us. I'm just the guy providing the snacks and switching cable channels every so often.

"What do you think?" She asks when she finishes the last one.

"They are pretty nice," I say, admiring each one. "You're pretty talented, woman."

She shrugs. "One more thing checked off of my list."

"You can't take a compliment, can you?" I reach out for her hand and squeeze it. "It's very simple. You just say thank you and be proud of your work."

"Thank you," she mouths bashfully.

I hate that she's uncomfortable, and I'm afraid that she might grab her stuff and leave. I tilt my head toward the balcony.

"It's nice outside," I say. "Why don't we take a wedding break, grab a few drinks, and kick back on the balcony."

"Sounds nice," she says. "Let me check on Max."

"He's still on top of the cupboards," I announce as I enter the kitchen. "He's a climber that one."

She doesn't respond. Grabbing a bucket with ice and a few beers, I head to the terrace where she's already sitting back and watching the city.

"Mind if I put on some music?" I ask when I set the bucket on the coffee table.

"I'd be insulted if you didn't," she jokes.

The first thing my playlist lands on is some lesser known Culture Club song. She seems to like it though, judging by the way she starts swaying her upper body while holding her beer bottle.

"I don't know if this is a dancing song..." I say.

"Any song's a dancing song if you try hard enough," she argues.

"I don't think that's right, but I don't know enough about dancing to undanceable music to dispute that," I joke.

She laughs, rises from her seat and holds her hand out to me. "Come on, I'll show you."

"Alright," I say. "I've always wanted to be led."

She doesn't really lead us so much as she leads until I've got enough rhythm that I can lead us myself. It's a process, but it works.

We're traipsing back and forth, throughout my entire balcony.

She's graceful, but not in a dainty way. She reminds me of a gymnast or a ballerina, lithe but so fucking powerful.

"Were you an acrobat in a past life?" I joke.

She snorts. "Nah. But I used to climb."

"Climbing?" Shit.

"Yeah, how else will I get around after the apocalypse?"

She's a climber, and she loves animals. *And* she's hilarious. That's just like—

Maybe she isn't perfect. She's just familiar because I'm an idiot who's still hung up on the idea of someone else.

Guess there's one way to test this.

"You ever been spelunking?" I ask.

She scrunches her nose. "Honestly, I hate caves. They scare the shit out of me."

"Same," I say enthusiastically. "They're so dark and narrow—"

"And jagged and what if you get trapped in there—"

"With the mole people—"

"Exactly!" she says.

"Everyone makes fun of me when I say that. They're always like 'You like climbing, what's the difference?' and as soon as I break out my mole people rationale," she says as she winks at me, "I've lost them."

"The difference is you can see in front of you," I explain logically. "And creepy shit is less likely to come up behind you and suck your brains out."

"You get it!" She claps and bounces on her feet a couple of times.

Welp, she was right. I'm an idiot who needs to stop comparing women.

She smiles at me like I'm a million bucks. Fuck, she's just perfect, isn't she?

She gets all the weird shit that makes me, well, me. She gets the 80s music and quipping jokes at every hour of the day. We spent all of last night whispering back and forth in different accents. She's practicing so when she can afford to travel the world, she can be a fake German tourist in Tokyo or whoever she wants to be that day.

She's just so—

"Jason!" Emmeline's voice causes all my dreams to come crashing to a halt. "I brought your records! Where are you?"

"Who's that?" Eileen asks.

"A nuisance," I say out loud, making sure Em listens.

There's no way I'm letting her come barging into my house, meeting my friends, and not giving her shit for it. What kind of future brother-in-law does she think I am?

"Because giving your shit back is, bad?" Em, who has the hearing of a bat, asks.

"No, no, this isn't an innocent house call," I say as I head back inside. "You're snooping."

And wouldn't you know—I find Emmeline in the kitchen looking at the paint drying on Eileen's signs.

"Gorgeous," she says, examining them. "Who made them?"

"Uh, me, duh," I lie as I search for her other half. "Where is he?"

Em shoots me an unimpressed look. I sigh.

"Eileen, she likes your work," I shout.

Eileen comes running in. She slows down at the very last second when she gets in Em's sightline. Trying to be casual, I can appreciate that.

"Really?"

Em's face does this thing. She looks us both over before saying "These signs are gorgeous. Did you do them yourself?"

Eileen blushes. "Yeah I did, thanks."

"What firm are you with?" Em asks sliding into her professional mode.

"Leave her alone," I warn Em, the same time as Eileen asks, "Firm?"

"She's asking if you work for a graphic design or marketing firm," I clarify.

Emmeline clears her throat and crosses her arms.

I roll my eyes. "Em, this is Eileen. Sister of the bride," I introduce them. "Eileen, this is Emmeline. My brother's..."

"*Girlfriend,*" Em says. "Sometimes Jason likes me. Today... not so much."

"You sorta just let yourself into my home," I remind her of this little thing called barging into my life because she's too damn nosy.

Em shrugs, basically ignoring me. She offers Eileen a handshake and says, "Seriously, this work is fantastic. I know some people who've been looking to hire a new designer."

Eileen blushes. "Thanks, but, it's more of a hobby."

Em nods. "Well if you ever want to work commissions, let me know. I could get you a project or two. Jason can forward you my information."

"I will, thanks," she says.

They exchange a few more pleasantries, which is so fucking weird it makes my head explode. They're just two different parts of my world right now. It feels like Eileen is being taken away from me.

Which is stupid. I don't own her. There's just something special about us spending time together.

Alone.

Without either of our families in the way.

It seems like they get along, though. It eases the tightness in my chest. But I just don't want this to become the beginning of my family butting into whatever is happening right now. Whatever is happening right now between Eileen and me.

I can see it already. June taking a flight from wherever she is in the world. Alex will RSVP for the wedding just to get a closer look. Next will be Jeannette, and my parents won't be that far away.

Nosy, meddling people who just can't let me enjoy the moment. Still, I'm grateful for my flock.

"Jason, walk me out, will you?" Em says a few minutes later.

"She nice," Em says when we get to the door.

I step into the hallway, closing the door behind us so Eileen won't hear.

"Yeah," I agree, shoving my hands in my pockets. "She is."

"And she thinks you're nice," Em continues.

I shrug my shoulders.

The fucking truth of the matter is, even if I'm willing to admit she's something I didn't know could exist—that doesn't mean she'll think I'm worth a damn.

After all these years I can still hear those words, *not with you*. I've created a life for myself where I can *be* only for me. This is who I am, how I like to live my life. I don't need to show anyone if I'm worth shit, do I?

Em hums. "You're an idiot."

I scowl at her. "Thanks, that makes me feel all fuzzy inside."

"This thing you call life is a journey," she says. "It's about growing and changing. You come to terms with your past, with who you were and what you are. You learn to let go and begin to love again."

And once again, Em thinks she's the smartest person on the planet. Which... "Does your sage wisdom come with SparkNotes or do you get a kick out of being cryptic?"

She smirks, crossing her arms. "A little, but what I'm saying is what if she's actually the person who saves you from living alone for the rest of your life?"

Fuck this again. "Could we have one conversation where you don't act like I'm some sad charity case you have to fix?"

"Maybe I'm just being selfish," she counteracts. "What if all this is just about making sure that my guy isn't worried about his kid brother fucking around when he's worth more than he thinks?"

My jaw ticks. Her words sting.

"You're better than who you try to be," she lets her shoulders fall dramatically.

"So, what now? Will you hand me another fortune cookie to fix me?"

Em sighs. "It's up to you, Jason. You're the only person who can make *you* happy."

She stares at my front door. "She could help you, though. If you let her."

I shrug, letting her walk off in frustration. I'm sure I'll get a call from Jack later tonight about how I annoyed "the love of his life." But I just don't care right now.

Em doesn't get it. Then again, maybe I don't either.

28

Eileen

Two days before the wedding

RAIN POURS DOWN MY FACE. Overhead, thunder roars. The wind knocks against my coat and bag as I run.

I can't anymore.

I have to get away.

This day has been the worst. Jason and I spent the entire morning running around, shuttling the wedding party to their hotel rooms and doing last minute outfit checks. Then we had to keep them entertained while also handling a catering snafu.

Who leaves the seafood outside the refrigerator overnight?

Mom blamed me. I hired the wrong caterer. If I had hired Amanda like Charlie had requested this wedding would be on track.

It didn't even matter that Charlie demanded peonies in the flower arrangements. Not just any peonies. White blush pink. Of course, she had to take my favorite flowers from me too.

But it was fine because things were going *smoothly*.

154 • CLAUDIA BURGOA

We were in the clear. Things were finally coming together. We sent the last of the party favors with the bridesmaids to finish. Thank fuck Charlie's real friends are more reliable than she is.

And then Jason had to open his big fucking mouth.

"Your birthday's coming up right?"

That's the straw that broke my fucking back. I'm so tired of everything—of my family shitting on me, of being overworked and underappreciated, and of nothing I do ever being good enough to make a difference. I'm so sick of living this shitty life where no one thinks of me, and I just have to take it.

Even when I beg them to listen.

So, I finally do something I never done in my life.

I run.

Jason's voice calls after me for a while.

"Eileen, wait, what's happening?" He yells, his voice distorted by the sound of the pouring rain. "Sweetheart, stop."

Eventually it fades. I think he got the message. I'm better off not dealing—

"Hey, wait," Jason says as he catches my hand.

Dammit, I think as I turn around and find him too close to me.

His hair wet, drops pouring down his face but the intensity on his whiskey colored eyes make my heart skip several beats. But I shove away the fluttering butterflies that swirl around every time he is near.

What's the point of being attracted to someone who is about to fade?

"How are you so fucking fast!"

"I'm taller!" He shouts, more panicked than upset. "Now will you tell me what's wrong?"

I shrug. What's the point in talking about me?

"I upset you." He isn't asking but stating.

"It doesn't matter," I say.

"Of course it does! Look at me, Eileen," he says.

I stare up at his big beautiful brown eyes and the pained expression he has on his face.

It guts me.

He's upset.

"What? Why does it even matter?"

"Because you're hurting," he says, licking his lips. "Can we please talk about it?"

What's the use in talking about it?

No one ever listens. Nor fucking cares what I think, or feel, or what happens to me. Except for Camilla. She's the only one who would care what's going on with me, and I can't even reach her.

No one else gives a fuck about me.

Even if they did, I honestly doubt they know how to think about anyone but themselves.

It's been years and years of trying to get my family to listen, trying to get them to forgive, and for what?

For making sure Charlie finished high school. For not pushing my help on her when she wanted to find her own way? Even then it doesn't matter because there's always another reason to be angry at me, or disappointed.

They can't live with me, but fuck me if I'm not on call to wait on them hand and foot.

My entire life is swarming in mangled, unrequited relationships.

So why does Jason want to be any different?

"Why do you care?" I ask, maybe even whimper.

He takes a step forward. We're inches apart. He puts his hands on my shoulders, squeezing lightly. He opens his mouth, the immediately snaps it shut. He does that a few more times.

Jason's eyes are so sad but so sincere.

It's like he's trying to say something, but the words aren't coming.

For some reason, it reminds of a few days ago. We were in my favorite antique shop and I was trying to tell him not to give up on his dreams. He asked me the same thing.

Why do you even care?

My breath catches. I know what I wanted to say.

He's the only thing that's made me happy in a really long time. Of course, I care if he's even an ounce as happy as he's made me.

Suddenly, my body just reacts, hugging him tightly. He hugs me back, just as tight.

He feels so safe. Like... like a home I wish I knew.

Rain masks my tears as Jason's arms shield me from the bullshit of the world. Part of me thinks I can't trust him, or anyone for that matter.

There's no point in making myself vulnerable to someone else.

He hums an old love song under his breath. I don't know if he does it for his sake or mine. Regardless, it makes me think maybe he isn't someone or just another person.

Maybe he's the only person who's ever cared enough to matter.

"My birthday," I mumble, letting the words out, the resentment.

The anger that's been brewing in my gut for the past two weeks.

"I'm planning her fucking wedding for my birthday," I explain further. Each word tastes like bile. "My graduation day. Because Charlie doesn't give a fuck about anyone else! She doesn't care. None of them do."

If she hadn't been pregnant, I would've been traveling alone to Aruba. *Happy Birthday, pathetic loser.*

Jason hugs me tighter.

We stand there, hugging in the rain, for another minute or so. It feels like we're the only people in existence.

"You wouldn't happen to have an umbrella in that giant purse of yours?" he asks, not letting me go.

I shake my head.

"You're kidding?"

"It barely rains in this forsaken desert," I say with a chuckle.

He laughs. It makes my nerves bubble up into laughter. He's good at making the unbearable wonderful.

"Wanna find somewhere drier?" he asks. "I know a place up the road, and I think you literally owe me a raincheck on drinks."

I smirk, squeezing one last time before I let him go.

"Lead the way," I say.

29

Eileen

THE RAIN'S pounding so hard on us that my back feels like it's getting a complimentary massage, courtesy of the same thing that's ruining my hair. I can barely see the hand Jason's pulling me with into this bar of his.

I don't get a good look at anything until we're sitting in a dry booth at the corner of this place. I use some paper towels Jason gives me to dry my hair. Thankfully my purse is waterproof or I'm sure all of our last minute notes on the wedding would be ruined.

Not that Charlie would notice. As long as things look perfect enough for her, she doesn't care what people had to go through to make them happen.

"Drink," he says, putting a shot of whiskey in front of me.

I knock it back without thinking. "Give me another," I say.

He slides one toward me as he gets up, "I'll grab some more. Can't have you getting trashed by yourself."

Jason brings a tray with two shot glasses and a bottle of single malt. I swallow hard. This is out of my league. I'm a beer, cooler and casual tequila drinker. Not that I haven't tried hard liquor, but I don't drink it often.

Not by the bottle.

The next shot goes down smoother than the first. Fuck, he paid for the good shit. I'm too tired to feel guilty or ask how much he wants me to give towards the tab. I just want to forget everything. My sister, my parents, my career, and that stupid wedding in two days.

I take a deep breath, letting my eyes adjust to this bar. The tables are scratched and the green vinyl booth seats look like they need reupholstering. Wait a second—

In the corner of my eyes I notice an all too familiar neon sign.

"We're in Finley's," I say.

"Uh, yeah?" Jason says as he sits down across from me. "You ever been here before?"

"This was my dad's pub," I say, gesturing wildly at some of the decorations. "I come here every week. See? Josh the bartender is waving at me."

I wave back as Josh shouts, "Didn't know you were friends with Spearman!"

"It's a recent development," I shout back.

Jason takes a double shot as he pushes a glass of water my way.

"You're fucking with me," he says. "I've been coming here every week since I found this place six months ago, and I've never seen you here."

"I come here on Tuesdays for half-priced pints," I say.

He groans, "Lame. I only have time to come on Sundays for trivia."

I nod. "Makes sense. I got banned from trivia."

He crooks an eyebrow. "Because..."

"...My best friend and I won three months in a row," I say sheepishly.

He laughs. It sounds half shocked, half hysterically enthused.

"How are you a real person? You're so fucking incredible it should be illegal."

"I'm not," I say, blushing.

"Sure, be humble," he says and winks. "Your secret is safe with me, genius."

The glint in his eyes is so hard to read. I chalk it up to a drinking haze. I keep chugging some water, so I don't die later. Wouldn't that be ironic? My mother yelling over my tombstone that I ruined Charlie's big day.

Bitch.

I cover my face and look around.

There it is. The first stages of being drunk. My filters begin to disappear. I should stop while I'm ahead.

What if I reach the *wildly drastic* stage of drunkenness?

"They pay me nothing. I earned more while I worked here as a bartender during my master's degree," I explain to him. "As if having a college degree, two master's degrees and a doctorate is nothing but bullshit."

I drink more water after the fourth, or maybe fifth shot.

"It'd be fine if I were paid enough to be comfortable," I say sighing.

"So work in a private practice," Jason argues.

"No," I say. "I can't do that to the kids who really need it."

"You ever think that maybe if you made enough to survive through a private practice, you could work with low income families within their means?"

I slump back in my chair. "Huh."

"Gotcha there, didn't I? Break the system, don't let it break you," he says with a triumphant smirk.

And then Jason goes on a rant about the Bee Gees—

"I'm just saying, they killed disco," he says.

I laugh. "Because disco needed help dying?"

We get distracted... a lot. Or maybe I can't keep track of the conversation. Am I drunk?

I clear my throat, trying to act casual as I reintroduce this sore topic. "So, if I can go after my dreams—why won't you?"

Jason takes a swig of beer. "Wanna do Irish car bombs?"

I narrow my gaze. No, it's not me. He's diverting the conversation and avoiding what I tell him.

"I will if you stop trying to derail this conversation," I say.

He gets up. He smirks as he leads me to the bar, saying "We'll see."

Irish car bombs are weird. Not because you're supposed to drink them before they curdle, but because I've never been able to tell when they do.

Maybe a part of me doesn't understand when good things are ruined, or I have no sense of self-preservation. Something like that.

"You're really bad at those," he says when he finishes first.

I shrug. "I could easily take a tequila shot better than you."

"Honestly, I'd rather not die that way," he confesses.

I hum, closing my eyes. "How would you die? If you could choose?"

"Easy. I'd go out in front of a live audience. Sing my swan song and then croak off like an instantaneous heart attack or something," he says.

"Poetic, but morbid," I say. "It suits you."

"You?" he asks.

I shrug. "Probably something mundane like choking."

"Ouch. What? Nothing cool?"

I roll my eyes. "We don't all have to be as interesting as you."

"You're the most interesting person on the planet," he says. "I think you deserve to go out in style."

I blush.

Somewhere around six drinks, we start arguing about what matters in life. *Happiness.*

How it depends on the quality of life and your thoughts. He disagrees about the concept.

"I don't get what the big deal is," Jason says. "It isn't objective. Everyone from Oprah to James Corden exist to entertain you, make you laugh, and maybe give you a tip or two. But not everyone agrees with all of them. It's the same with being happy."

"That doesn't even make sense." I claim. "I agree. It's subjective but also, like love, it exists—even when you can't see or touch it."

"Love doesn't give you happiness," he says with a gruff voice.

"The fact is that you act like you don't deserve to be happy," I argue.

He glances at me, taking a swig of the beer he's been nursing for a while and says, "Hey kettle, ever seen a mirror before?"

"Don't start with me—" I say, my jaw tightening.

"We're in a bar, *literally* drinking our troubles away because your sister is so selfish, she had to steal your birthday," he argues, like a lawyer showing the jury the most powerful evidence to close his case. "The least you could do is stop wallowing in self-pity and do something about it."

My laugh comes out cold and flat. "Hey pot, why don't you get off your fucking high horse and accept you're lonely and kinda hate yourself for giving up on yourself for money."

"Fuck you," Jason says, between sips of beer. "I did what I had to do to keep go—"

"You are a romantic!" I shout over the blaring music. "You're just so fucking scared of getting your heart broken again you're just wasting your life away doing *nothing*!"

He spits out some of his beer. "I'm scared? You're so fucking scared of upsetting or disappointing your family you don't do anything for yourself!"

"At least I don't shut my family out—"

"Because they crush you! Every fucking day!" He claims.

I think I'm about to slap him when I notice the Queen song that's playing. Which, by drunk logic, takes precedence.

"Fuck," I say, sighing contently. "I love this song."

He laughs, the tension melting out of his shoulders. "It's the fucking best."

"Right?" I say, unaffected by how my words are starting to slur more. "It's like the perfect song—"

"To get lost in when all you need is a *win*," he says. "The underdog, searching for just the right moment to swoop in and make your dreams a reality."

It's insane how much he gets me. It's too good to be true.

"I love how you get me too," he says.

Shit, I said that out loud.

I get up, stumbling over to his side of the booth, scooting him over.

In no time, I start singing at the top of my lungs.

His smile is like the brightest star in the sky. Then, he starts harmonizing with me.

I can't tell if it's the drunkenness or our combined competitiveness, but we hold the note in *Somebody to Love* for an absurdly long amount of time.

Everything just melts away. It's me and him—those big beautiful eyes, that wonderful voice, this kind soul who found me in a sea of angry mediocrity, even with his wounds and mild cynicism.

He keeps singing.

"How are you so perfect?" I ask.

And single, I think. A man like him should be cherished and loved by someone who can see his value.

"Excuse me?" he says. "You're the most amazing person on the face of the earth. I can't believe you haven't been there every day of my entire life."

"It feels like I have," I mutter. "Like we've been doing this—thing —forever. You're just so smart and funny—"

"—No, fuck no, that's you," he insists. "And you can sing! How do you not know how fucking amazing you are?"

"Takes one to know one," I say. "Oh shit, this is my favorite part."

He sings, and as he follows Freddy's voice, I believe he wants to leave the passion cell, as much as I know that someday, I will finally be free. So, I join him.

The music crescendos slowly. His lips are moving. I can't pay attention to much else.

"For what it's worth," he says suddenly. "I'm sorry I was an ass about your family. You're the kindest person I've ever met."

"I'm sorry I said you were too chickenshit to be happy. You're the most courageous person I've ever met," I say earnestly, licking my lips. "And you're probably stupidly fantastic at kissing."

He leans over, his lips press firmly against mine. He catches my top lip between his teeth, teasing it.

At first, it's just a brush from his warm lips that zings my skin and sears my mouth. I open for him. Our tongues get tangled together as my arms find their way around his neck. His hands slide up to frame my face, and he tilts my head, deepening the kiss.

I dig my nails in as this kiss becomes everything.

It's fireworks. Somersaults. It's a summer sunset and the first snowfall. It's the last time I went swimming as a kid. It's climbing the highest peak.

It's coming home after a lifetime away. It's a thousand lifetimes leading up to this one, simple resolution.

It's one soul calling out to another through an infinite abyss.

It's something like love.

The song ends. Our lips barely part. He stares at me with dilated pupils.

"See?" I say, still catching my breath. "Like that."

30

Eileen

I SHOULD BE HOME RIGHT NOW, I think to myself.

The rest of me is still singing *Somebody to Love* at the top of her lungs without giving a shit that I have to wake up early tomorrow morning. Instead, I grab a rideshare with Jason. We planned on doing two stops. But as we continued frantically kissing on our way to his place, I just couldn't leave.

And here I am, at his too big for one geek of an apartment. I smirk and look at him from head to toe.

"This was a night to remember," I say, thinking about the searing kiss, but not wanting to discuss it.

Why spoil this night with something as mundane as you kissed me like no one has ever before, so instead I tease him. "I can't believe you jumped on a table when Time After Time came on. I can't believe that table didn't *break* when you started dancing."

"Can't you, though?" He glares at me, but with that goofy grin on his delicious mouth. I don't believe he's upset. "Cindy Lauper is an icon."

"That's my song," I protest. "Josh said you sang it better than I do."

"So what's my prize then?"

I shrug. "Nothing."

"Do you seriously not get how fucking amazing you are?" He asks out of nowhere. "You never answered the question."

His hands cup my face, and our eyes meet. I don't breathe as he runs his palms down my neck and my arms until he holds my hands, his eyes never leaving mine.

"You're fucking beautiful." And when he says it, I want to believe it.

No, I *do* believe it.

Today, I'm just a girl who was kissed by the most handsome man in the land.

"You're fun and smart too," he says with a throaty voice.

He places a hand on the back of my neck, peering down at me. His eyes search mine. They shine and brighten more as he smiles.

He licks his lips. I can feel them approaching my own. My head screams he's about to kiss me again. And my heart beats fast as he leans closer and closer.

My insides twist and I can't think straight anymore. There's a pull between us, or maybe it's his strong palm pressing against my skin, closing the gap between us. When his lips brush against mine, I liquify into a puddle of want.

It's different from our first kiss. This one is urgent. My heart feels like it's about to burst. He devours me with his mouth and my skin aches for his touch. We don't speak.

Our hands are busy undoing each other's clothing while our mouths can't seem to get enough to satiate our appetite for each other.

He stops kissing. I almost whimper missing his mouth already.

"Do you want this?" He asks and his face is pretty serious.

Leave. There's a voice drowned out by all the alcohol I consumed tonight.

I'm not drunk, but sober enough to know what I'm doing but with enough buzz to let myself get lost in his arms.

How many times have I been with a caring man like Jason?

I push away the warning because today I'm taking what I deserve, what I want. Not in a million years will I allow myself to let my guard down. Today, I'm letting myself feel.

Instead of answering his question, I link my hands on the back of his neck and press myself against his bare, muscular chest. I grow bold and wild as our kiss becomes frantic. He slips his large hand between my legs, his rough fingers tracing my tender slit.

I can't believe it. Tossing caution to the wind isn't my MO. But here I am, letting a man who I just met a few weeks ago touch me in a way I've never been touch. Saying something I never thought I would, "Fuck me."

Greediness slams against my chest. I want him.

As his fingers play along my clit, I shudder and he lifts me by the waist, setting me on top of the couch. He lowers his head to my breasts, his lips sucking gently at the tip of my hard nipple. I whimper as he pinches my other pearl with the same intensity. My tits grow painfully swollen as he continues the ministration.

This is all too much but also too good.

The buzz of the alcohol disappears, but the high on him increases as his fingers skim down my stomach and find my center.

"Yes," I gasp.

He plunges two fingers inside my core.

"First, I'm going to make you come with my mouth," he warns me with that joking tone I love.

Then he pulls his digits out giving room for his tongue. He licks me with one long stroke from my vulva to my entrance making me squirm. His thumb strokes my clit slowly as his other fingers make their way inside me.

I whimper one more time when instead of two, he dips in three fingers, stretching me wider. His thumb teases my clit.

He alternates between sucking my clit, plunging his fingers or pushing his tongue inside me. I moan, my eyes close as he continues devouring me with his mouth, hard and fast. Every nerve ending is tightened into a knot.

I'm desperate. Lust rushing through my veins like adrenaline. I can't get enough and he's not giving me enough. I want nothing more than to come, with him inside me.

When I open my eyes, I find his intense gaze on me. I can't take everything at the same time. The frantic movement of his mouth and fingers along with those devouring eyes. Then suddenly, and without warning, I come undone.

It's a blissful moment. Ripples go through every cell of my body as I travel up to the stars and back.

That's when he stands, and I see him. Tall, chiseled like a Michelangelo, naked and my eyes can only focus on his erect manhood. It's swollen, long and thick. Impressive. I want it inside me.

He rolls over a condom and steps in between my legs. The tip of his cock set right against my slit.

His eyes don't leave mine as he pushes himself inside me, slowly. Thrusting every inch carefully as I adjust to his size. The connection between us is palpable. We can't get enough of each other. Once he is all the way in, his mouth takes mine.

And this is happening. I'm letting go of any worries and allowing myself to just feel pleasure. I let the fire consume me. Burn me to the ground as our pace becomes frantic and urgent.

"More," I beg. "Faster."

I don't want for this to end, yet, I want to reach the highest mountain and let myself burst into flames.

We both tense at the same time. He swears with a guttural voice.

I gasp for air, wanting more.

31

Eileen

One day until the wedding

I WAKE up at the crack of dawn to the sound of a television playing. It's that time of spring when the sun's already out, despite it being too early for decent human beings to be awake. The light is like a pick-ax against my brain.

I guess we went hard. It takes me a minute to sober up enough to get my bearings. I'm in a bedroom that isn't mine. The other side of the bed is empty, but still warm. Shit, what did I do last night?

I vaguely remember doing karaoke with Jason. We were arguing about... disco? There was more arguing, and I said too much about how great he is—

"Fuck," I say under my breath.

We kissed. We made out at Finley's of all places. If this gets back to Dad, my parents will kill me.

"Shit, okay," I tell myself. "It's fine."

Just have to deny, deny, and deny. Maybe I can get Jason to go along with that. It's not like he actually wanted to have sex with me. We were drunk, caught up in the heat of the moment.

Not that drunk, you knew what you were doing. I remind myself.

That's not the point. Let's put the dots on the i's and lines on the t's.

He wouldn't want me for more than a one-night stand. He's a playboy. Even if he wanted to change who he is, he is way too sophisticated and charming to want to settle for *me*.

I take a few deep breaths. There's an aspirin and water on the bedside table, thank fuck. I'm naked save for this old *Rocky Horror Picture Show* t-shirt that's draped over my body like a dress.

Definitely went home with Jason.

Following the sound of the television, I find him sitting on the couch watching the news.

"Any high speed chases?" I say as I approach the couch.

He chuckles. "No, just reviewing some hearing the senate committee on health, education, labor, and pensions had yesterday."

"Oh," I say as I settle down next to him.

Without looking away from the screen, he hands me his coffee mug. I take a sip.

"This blend is so good. Where did you get it?" I mumble.

"Specially delivered from Seattle," he informs me.

"That's so wasteful," I say.

"And yet, so delicious," he adds.

I groan into the cup. "I would sell my soul for another cup of this."

"Well, hang on," Jason says as he gets up. "No need to sell your soul. I'll make another cup. You can finish that one."

I watch him as he goes to the kitchen—shirtless with disheveled hair and flannel pajama pants. Even his back muscles are corded. The need and craving stir inside my gut and my legs clench as the ache between them pulses.

Maybe he'd be up for another round if I beg?

Fuck, I would give anything for one more round with him. But it can't happen. My parents would disown me. Charlie would have a conniption about how I'm "upstaging her wedding."

Jason gives me a soft, familiar smile as he approaches the couch.

He's also the first friend I've had in a long time who really gets me. Camilla loves me, but she indulges most of my hobbies. Jason gets me and appreciates what I'm into and who I am.

I don't think I could handle losing that, or him.

Sipping the coffee he gave me, I take a shuddering breath. I could just ask.

Yeah, what a great idea, I think sarcastically.

How shall I start?

"Hey Jason, I know you're completely out of my league, but what if we ran away together and never saw my family again?"

No, I can up that with a better line. "What if we moved to some tiny corner of New York, set up shop, and built a life together?"

He'd never go for something as crazy as that. Why would I even go out of state when I love this place so much? Because if I go there, no one would shatter my happiness. Not that he is it.

Still, I have to say something though. Friends don't just wake up in each other's beds wearing each other's sleep clothing casually.

Jason, mercifully, starts talking about the committee hearing on TV. I throw some of my opinions at him, which isn't hard. The hearing directly concerned resources for neurodivergent kids. That's a topic I have personal stake as well as professional credentials to talk about it.

He has some aspirational ideals about the whole thing, but I appreciate his enthusiasm and energy. I didn't realize how jaded and cynical I've grown with this industry that I used to care so much about.

I really needed that vacation and definitely a pay raise.

"So..." I say eventually, finally biting the bullet. "About last night—"

"Yeah. It was crazy, right?"

"A little," I agree. "But I was wondering if you had any thoughts or opinions?"

"I don't know. I think you had some points about the Second British Invasion," he points out. "But I don't know if I can agree with your opinions on disco."

Normally I'd pick an argument about this discussion he's waving in my face. But this is something we should talk about.

"No, I mean—how much do you remember about last night?"

"Uh, gotta be honest, not much," he says, grimacing as he scratches the back of his neck.

"What's the last thing you remember?"

"Arguing about music," he says. "I vaguely remember karaoke, but not enough to tell you what we sang or what we did afterward."

He doesn't remember us sleeping together.

"Why?" Jason asks. "Do you remember something I don't."

This is my get out of jail free card. I'd be an idiot not to side step confronting us sleeping together.

I shrug, staring at my mug as I take another sip. "Nope, I was hoping you could fill in the blanks for me. I blacked out after the Irish car bombs."

He snorts. "Sorry, dude. I know about as much as you do."

We laugh together, like we always do. This time it doesn't feel comforting.

It's hollow and stiff. He's lying, and I'm following right behind. The back of my eyes fill with moisture. Because fuck, I'm just one more woman who slept in Jason's bed and gets to walk out without a thank you note.

That's good, isn't it. Hakuna Matata and all that shit. And we go back to watching the news, mumbling opinions on occasion.

This is a blessing I keep reminding myself. I wanted to deny everything, and now I can. I don't even have to take Jason's rejection. This is everything I wanted when I woke up this morning.

So why do I feel so shitty?

32

Eileen

THE REHEARSAL DINNER starts on time. The catering is good, our families are pleasant with each other. The speeches are short and surprisingly appropriate.

Great-Uncle Ernie doesn't try to steam the microphone at any point. Even Marek's dumbass friends keep themselves relatively sober.

Everything is right on schedule. Everything is going according to plan. Everything, except Jason. Other than when he gives his best man speech, I don't see him all night.

At one point, he texts me saying the kitchen almost ran out of our vegetarian option. Charlie's friends are so indecisive, I'm not surprised they pulled this. Then he added the question, should we order more vegetarian options for tomorrow?

The food doesn't matter. What does is his stupid behavior.

He is avoiding me.

Not to sound paranoid, but in the entire time I've known Jason, he's never been an avid fan of social gatherings and would rather stick close to a single person if possible. Well, he's not a fan of my family, and since most of his bailed, I can't understand his absence.

I run into his brother's girlfriend—who's with said brother. Jack seems quiet and nice.

But if Jason isn't with any of them, isn't with Marek, isn't with *Jossie* and her date, and isn't anywhere on the dancefloor, where the fuck is he?

Why would he be avoiding this event he's been so invested in?

Why has he up and disappeared right when everything's falling into place?

The only thing that's changed since yesterday when he was gung ho about being here and right now at the rehearsal dinner is *me*. I try to ignore his absence for a while, but it gets under my skin.

I don't even want to be here anymore. Charlie's whining every so often about how no one's paying attention to her.

Maybe if I hide in the storage closet I saw by the kitchen until the night wraps up...

I sneak my way around the head of the table, making excuses to go to the restroom. It takes a few minutes to get past some of the crowd and a few obligatory chats. When I finally get there, I open the door so carefully, sliding into the darkness quietly. I think part of me is worried I'll give away my potential hiding spot.

What really happens is I slide into the closet and bump into someone else who jabs me in the forehead with their elbow.

"Ow," I say. "What the fuck?"

"Eileen?" Jason's voice echoes slightly in the darkness.

"Yeah. Hi."

"What are you doing here?"

"Hiding from everyone else," I respond logically. "You?"

"Also hiding," he offers casually.

Great, we're back to pleasantries and nonsense. Wait, we never shared those. In the dark, I decide to confront him—again. A redo from this morning.

"From me," I supply.

"That's not—entirely true," he defends himself.

I yelp. "I knew it! You've been weird ever since we got here."

Actually, since I woke up in your bed, but let's not bring that up—yet.

"What gives?"

"I perhaps, potentially, remember some things that happened last night," he whispers.

"You lied earlier today," I supply.

He mumbles some nonsense.

"Sorry, I can't hear you," I whisper shout.

"Well," he clears his throat. "I just thought it would be better if I weren't out there making things awkward."

"Why don't you just say it as it is," I push him further. "You remember everything that happened last night!"

"Okay, guilty, I—wait a second, remember what?"

"Oh, you very well know—"

"As I recall," he says, his voice getting louder and pitchy, "Someone said they knew about as much as I did, which was supposed to be nothing."

I cross my arms, dumbfounded. "Well, to be fair, I was technically telling the truth."

He groans. "I can't believe you!"

"Me? Believe yourself! Why couldn't we have talked this morning like fucking adults."

There's an awkward pause before he sighs. "You're right. I know you're right. I'm sorry."

I sigh in relief. Okay, I can work with this.

"It was just a drunken hookup after all," he says, shattering my heart carelessly. "There's no shame in that."

I dust my chest, knowing that there's nothing salvageable from the debris. It's bound to happen. Naïve girl believes in a handsome, unusual, playboy asshole and he kicks you like a puppy.

But I have to save face.

"Of course not!" I say quickly. "Hooking up with a friend as a one-time thing? In this day and age? That's so not a big deal."

He does that fake laugh thing he always does around Charlie when he's ready to run for the hills.

"I don't know why I was worried," he says. "You get me, Eileen."

Swallowing thickly, I nod. And then I realize he can't see that, so I say, "Yeah."

After a moment he says, "You know it's also pretty normal to hook up with a friend multiple times in this day and age."

I have no idea what's his angle, but I'll take the lifeline he's giving. Anything to feel his lips on mine one more time.

The last round before we leave.

"You know, you're totally right," I say. "That's something reasonable adults could do."

"And if there's something we are, it's reasonable."

I swallow again. "Well... I'm game if you are."

Jason reaches out, tangling his fingers into my hair and tugging me against him. He crashes his lips against mine. I open, hungrily as his tongue pushes my lips. It's a kiss of two lovers who have been starving for centuries, when it's only been hours since he was inside me.

I whimper when he deepens the kiss. My hands holding onto his strong biceps, clinging to him as we hide in this tight space, running away from the outside and searching for a minute of peace. Or is it searching for each other's company. Fuck, how can I miss him when he's right here with me.

The only thing I know is that I want him raw, claiming my body, quieting the outside. Protecting me from every bad decision I've made that has put me in this place.

I just want him, branding me with his mouth. Claiming me. Setting my skin on fire with his hands.

Keeping me alive while I try to stay afloat.

My fingers fumble with his belt and his zipper while his hands roll up the skirt of my dress, his fingers shove my panties to the side and immediately begin rubbing against my clit. I'm breathing hard.

"It's been a long day," he says between breaths as I pull his cock free of his pants.

I run my hand along his thick, stiff length. I want to kiss it, swallow it. If I could, I would go down on my knees and suck it like I did last night. Make him come inside me.

He pushes me against the door of the closet.

"Fuck, I missed your body so damn much," he whispers in my ear as he reaches around my ass, squeezing it and lifting my body. "Wrap your legs around my waist."

I do as he says. He positions himself right at my entrance and pushes his cock deep inside me.

"Fuck," I grunt as he stretches me, fills me, and brings me back.

"If we were at home," he says, moving slowly. "I would bury my face between your legs until you scream out my name. This will have to do for now."

Oh god, it feels so good as he buries his dick deep inside me. One hand holds me, while the other finds my clit and begins to rub it. My head falls back. I close my eyes as he fucks me against the door, hard, roughly.

He growls, pushing himself further as I say, "Faster, deeper."

Ripples of pleasure throb between my legs as the ecstasy hits me hard. But he's not done so he continues pumping, thrusting himself inside me. My hands clench onto his shoulders. It's inexplicable how my body begins to convulse again, violently.

This is so good.

He swears under his breath and whispers my name in a low, guttural voice.

He is shaking, or maybe it's me.

He slides in and out slowly, as if he doesn't want this to end. Not just yet. We keep the connection as long as we can. But when he pulls out of me, I feel hollow, but there's a wedding rehearsal just outside the very door we just fucked against and the horror hits me at once.

I just had sex. In the closet. With my family only a few feet away.

As Jason pulls me to him, pressing my body tightly against his and kissing my temple, I'm shaken to my very core.

33

Eileen

I'M BACK at the scene of the crime. This time we're both sober and still craving each other as much as we were last night.

"Are you sure about this?" His warm breath caresses my hair.

I stifled a groan as his hands slide down my bare arms. His simple touch turns me on. His fingers touching the skin around my waist feel like fire burning me from the inside out. I'm always cautious with everything I do, but when it comes to his lips, his touch... I just want to surrender myself.

"Eileen." The sound of my name coming out from his lips is like a silken caress. I clench my legs as I feel a pulse of pleasure between them. "What are you *doing* to me?"

Jason slides his hand under my chin, lifting it and slightly tugging me against him. He kisses me on the mouth with heated, seeking lips. It's deep, branding my soul with his strong, demanding lips. My fingers curl into his chest as my breath catches in my throat.

He makes my heart beat faster, and I should run because this feeling absolutely terrifies me. But I also feel so alive, more alive than I have *ever* felt.

Jason tugs his mouth away and looks down at me. My hands slide down his belly toward his hips. I needed more than just this kiss. The aching throb between my legs continues to build just by the feel of his body, and how it perfectly molds against mine.

"You're overdressed," I mention with a low voice.

"We couldn't have that now, could we?" he says suggestively.

He pulls his sweater off. The shirt comes off next and he tosses it onto the floor. The jeans drop down to his ankles along with his boxers.

I stare at him open mouthed. He... There are no words to explain how handsome this man is. Broad shoulders. Narrow waist. Muscled arms.

Every inch of him corded, and his hard, erect cock is a sight I never want to forget. I wish I could keep this moment, or at least the memory of being with him, forever. If I could only choose a few to preserve in my heart after this is over. They would be the warmth of his body, the sound of his heartbeat, and his scent.

"Stay with me," he says, bringing me back into the now.

How could I be thinking of what's to come when I have his gorgeous body right in front of me?

I reach out and touch his thick length, tracing it with my fingertips.

"Now it's your turn," he says. "I've been wanting to rip this dress off you since you got dressed in the closet.

He reaches around me, fumbling with the zipper and letting it drop. "What do you want tonight?" He kisses the corner of my lips. His fingers unfastening my bra while the other hand is pushing my underwear down.

I stiffen and moan as two of his fingers plunge inside me.

"I can't get enough of you—uh, of this I mean," he says. "If I could, I'd listen to your throaty moans all day long."

His hand moves slow.

He's careful.

His warm lips meet mine. My eyes flutter closed at the sensation of his fingers stretching my insides and his tongue brushing against mine. Electricity runs down my spine.

We kiss fast, long and hard. My brain and my nerves are a knotted jumble of sensations I can't understand, but I want to experience them. His mouth kisses the corner of my mouth and runs down my jaw. He lowers his head. I gasp when his lips trace my breasts.

I shiver as he licks my swollen peaks and then takes one nipple into his warm mouth. Both of his hands are now kneading my globes. His long hard suck of my nipple unravels me and makes me frantic with passionate need.

Something inside me burns. He feels so new and yet familiar. I can't understand how being with him makes me feel free and yet bound to him. Though I crave his touch everywhere, I want him inside me desperately.

"I want more," I say between breaths.

"Hold on," he says gruffly, releasing my breasts.

He retrieves a condom, slipping it on with ease. He sits at the edge of the bed and says, "You're in charge."

I sip some air, letting it out as I take his hand and let him pull me on top of him. We sit down on the bed, his hard length pressing against my center. He kisses my bare shoulder pressing me tight against him. Then,he nips his way to my bottom lip, nibbling it and dipping his tongue into my mouth.

When his tongue meets mine, a throaty moan escapes me. I swear, I feel him smiling as he kisses me, but he never breaks contact.

Oh, but how much I love his tongue. It's teasing, playful and loving, just like him.

While we kiss, we move slowly so I end up on top of his granite shaft. I close my eyes and place my hands on his shoulders as we align our bodies. Slowly, I lower myself onto his erection.

I feel every inch of him filling me, stretching my insides until I've taken all of him inside me. Our gazes meet. His eyes are soft and tender. His expression vulnerable.

As he wraps his arms around my waist, I begin to move up and down. We find our rhythm, it's just so easy... we just click. His mouth captures one breast as I bounce on top of him. He flicks my hard pearl twice before sucking it hard.

Pleasure shoots through my entire body. He throbs inside me, and I tighten my muscles, clenching his cock, and enjoying his grunt in response.

Our movements become frantic. Our two bodies become one, soaring as we climb up a mountain. Together, we scream out one another's name in unison as we reach the peak and touch the furthest star in the galaxy.

The explosion suddenly tears me apart.

It's like nothing I've felt before. It feels like every good moment that's ever transpired has been leading up to this one.

He lays back onto the bed, his arms wrapping around me, pulling my body down with his. I'm boneless. Butter melted by the heat of his body. This... this is so good.

He's so good.

Maybe we can make this work out. Friends who fuck. Friends who sometimes see each other naked and don't have to consider anything deeper than that.

Maybe even friends who decide they're sick of looking for other friends and move in together and decide to be best friends forever.

I could live with being just his friend, if he'd let me.

I hear him whisper something, I'm just too tired to make out the words, and I fall into a deep sleep.

This will probably work out...

Maybe.

34

Jason

FOR ONCE, I don't wake up at the ass crack of dawn. The first thing I see is Eileen lying beside me. My arms wrapped around her. Last night comes back like a sucker punch to the gut.

Fuck, those kisses, the way her body responds to my touch. She's just everything. She's so fucking amazing, and the little sex we've had together is better than anyone I've ever been with. Hell, it's better than *anything* I have ever experienced.

I think I could spend forever here, like this, with her— well, not exactly here because we definitely need to shower at some point. But something like this would be nice.

Still, I can't believe she woke up to watch the news with me. It's the stuff dreams are made of. Okay, it's the stuff my dreams are made of.

A little minor detail decides to rear its ugly head my way. I told Eileen we could hookup as friends, right after I spent all day avoiding her and pretending I didn't remember any of the night before.

Shit, shit, fuck! Why am I so stupid?

She gave me plenty of chances to say something, change my

stupid mind. But I avoided her. Sometimes, avoiding reality seems like an easy fix until you fuck up what has become the most important relationship of your life.

She brought the fucking conversation up herself. Why didn't I take that opportunity?

Because admitting I have feelings would mean giving her full permission to reject me, break my heart, and crush my soul, I recall.

Right, shit. I'm fucked.

What am I supposed to do now? Fuck her for the rest of the weekend and then part ways? Keep her as a booty call until she gets sick of my bullshit and leaves? Or whatever the third option is that I can't think of right now?

I wonder if faking amnesia is an option.

Why Eileen? I ask silently, looking at her.

What did you do?

No, the question is what did I allow myself to do?

Okay, deep breaths Spearman. You've been in stickier situations with more to lose before.

Something in me wonders if there's anything bigger, anything that could top losing Eileen? Fuck, I wish I could slap myself right now. This is terrible. I should be able to talk myself out of this bullshit but—

Jossie, that's it!

All I have to do is get Jossie to shake the feelings out of me. She'll tell me I'm screwing up my life for someone who's a statistical risk, make me see all of Eileen's flaws, and then I can move on with my life.

That was Jackson's job, until Miss Emmeline came to his life, and now he wants the entire world to experience the ray of sunshine he gets to bask in every fucking day.

I look at Eileen, wondering if she is the warmth I need to keep me alive.

Easy boy, now you're being poetic and shit?

Lose her before she kicks you to the curb and stomps on your heart. The other one broke me. Eileen can destroy me completely.

But in the mean time I might as well enjoy the moment. I reach over and pull her to me. She groans softly, opening one eye and giving me a pleased smile.

"Morning, sleepy head," I greet her.

She blinks a couple of times and moans.

Oh fuck, don't do that. Just the sound makes me hard. Makes me want to be inside her. I brush her loose curls away and cup her face, connecting our gazes.

"Hey," she whispers as I brush my lips against her forehead and kiss her nose.

I can't remember what day today is. All I want is to stay in bed memorizing every inch of her body. Searing this moment into my mind before we say goodbye. As wonderful as it would be to wake up next to her everyday, I know it's impossible.

Who knows what I would do to fuck her up and make her run far away. I only know that it's a certainty that would happen.

So I do what I know. Stay in the moment. I unleash the beautiful sound of her moans as I make my way down her body, licking every freckle, birthmark and scar I find on my way down her gorgeous body. I part her thighs and slip my fingers along her wet heat. She groans and I kiss her with hunger.

There's no better way to wake up or any place than I rather be.

Starting my day as I lose myself in the kiss and her body. Eileen moves her leg on top of my hip and positions the tip of my cock right at her tender entrance. She's so fucking wet, I slide inside, feeling her walls spasm around my thick length as I stretch her channel.

"Fuck, if I could live buried inside you," I whisper, hugging her body and rolling so I end up on top of her.

We stare at each other, and I wonder who will be the lucky man. The lucky man who will win this woman's heart?

She's perfect in so many ways. Who knew Eileen McBean would be fun, intelligent and great in bed?

"You're thinking," she says, running her soft fingers along my jaw. "Stop. It's so loud."

"Just let it all go," she mutters, her voice so low I can barely hear her.

I slow down my pace as I get lost in her eyes, moving lazily in and out of her heat. Softly, reverently, the way she deserves it.

There's no urgency to end this. I stare into her eyes.

Soft, understanding and dangerously honest.

I could get lost in them forever.

What I would give to just *be* with this woman. Eileen smiles softly at me, and that smile just sucks all the air out of my lungs when she gives it just to me.

There are no words between us, just the air surrounding us as we continue melting into each other. The music around us is composed by our moans and the sound of our bodies as we move in soft circles grinding against each other.

If I ever thought about a perfect moment, this might be it.

I'm at the edge of the abysm but holding onto a thread before I let the pleasure take me away. I'm savoring the moment, letting it sink in as the last time we will be together like this. Allowing the sizzling electricity to sear every cell of my body, transforming them.

Whatever I become after she leaves will be happier than the man she found. I'll have the memories of her to keep me company, and I can't imagine a better treasure to carry in my heart.

Don't think, she mouths.

I give her a smile and continue. I would give her anything she asks right at this moment. My fortune, my heart, my entire life. Me.

Losing myself, I follow the rhythm of her body. She shutters and I know she's close. My hand finds her sweet, swollen clit and I begin to rub circles around it while thrusting faster.

I want to hear her cry with ecstasy. Remember how great this can be for her. That receiving is also gratifying. If I can only give her more than just this moment.

Her cries echo through the room. Her body twisting under mine as my own orgasm takes over me and I shudder on top of the most amazing woman I've ever met.

35

Jason

"HAPPY BIRTHDAY TO YOU," I sing, while I carry the vanilla cupcake I got her yesterday. "Happy birthday dear Eileen, happy birthday to you."

"Blow out the candle," I encourage her, but add, "Don't forget to make a wish."

She blows the candle and stares at the cupcake, then smiles at me.

"I didn't forget," I tell her and grin. "We were just, you know, *occupied* earlier."

She rubs her eyes. "Thanks."

"What?" I ask as I sit down to finish my breakfast.

For a beat I stare at her, scared that I missed something. Maybe I misunderstood and it was yesterday.

Fuck!

She shrugs and looks out the window facing away from me. It's not quick enough for me to miss that she starts crying. I rush over to take her in my arms, absorbing the sadness emanating out of every pore of her body.

"What's wrong, baby?" I whisper.

She shakes her head. "It's no—fuck, I'm just so tired, Jason."

I think on some level I didn't expect her to answer with how cagey she was acting. That's the only explanation for how I react.

"What? I—what?" I stutter.

"I know it's dumb," she says, sniffling. "But you know how long it's been since my parents gave a fuck about my birthday. Or me for that matter? They only agreed to go on vacation with me because I *begged* for *years*. Or I guess they didn't really agree to go with me. They never even bought their plane tickets. They just wanted me to stop pestering them so they gave the illusion that we would finally be going away *together*."

I hug her tighter. "What is their problem? Like, for real, what slimy insect crawled up their asses that they treat Charlie like a queen but you they can't even remember your birthday?"

She hiccups through a sob. "It got worse after I got Charlie kicked out of college."

"Say what," I say.

36

Eileen

Nine years ago

"CHEATING," my mother shouts. "Not only was she kicked out for poor attendance and failing grades, she was under review by the university for suspected plagiarism."

I've never seen her so angry before in my entire life. When she called me into her bedroom, she snapped at me to sit down and then spent the first ten minutes stomping back and forth. She keeps growling menacingly.

My dad sits silently in his recliner in the corner of the room. It was his dad's chair originally. It creaks with any sudden movement, whining louder than when Sam was a baby and couldn't sleep through the night.

Occasionally, Dad will take a sip of his beer. But it's been dead silent since my mom told me to sit down.

Until she just started shouting at me a moment ago.

"She said they dropped that last year," I argue quietly.

My mom glares as if to say, *now is not the time.*

I shut up.

"She had perfectly good grades in high school," she rants. "Top of her class."

That was me, not Charlie.

"She's smart," I say, staring at my feet.

"So doing her assignments, writing her notes that she could use for participation points—you had absolutely nothing to do with that?"

I swallow thickly. "I—"

"Her admissions essay." My mom is practically in tears at this point. "That beautiful piece on belonging and community involvement that made your father cry. That was—"

"It was true! I talked to her before I wrote it—"

"I'm done with your lies, Eileen," she says, indignantly. "Thanks to you, we've wasted a year and a half on tuition. Years of her education are gone. You've made your sister completely useless."

No, Mom, that was you.

I stare down at my sneakers. They're covered in sharpie from that night a few years ago when Charlie tried to sneak into the house while high on molly. I took her to the park and let her draw on my shoes until she sobered up more. It was a miracle we didn't get caught.

I fight back the urge to point out that Charlie's read everything I've ever given her. At least, that's what I think. In her defense, she got good scores on tests because we'd study together. She could explain things so well once she got the gist of a concept.

She isn't useless. Charlie needs a little push, not a hovering mother trying to solve her life or finding someone to solve her life.

She just hates school. Hates how hard it is to focus or sit still.

"I'm sorry," I say quietly. "I didn't mean—"

"It doesn't matter what you meant, Eileen," my dad finally says something. "It wasn't your call. You've ruined your sister's life."

I guess I did.

I didn't mean to ruin anything. I was just trying to help her, but she flunked out of school. It'll take forever to get her to graduate somewhere else. That's assuming she wants to go back to school.

"So now what?" I say, worried for Charlie but also scared shitless for myself.

These two are going to make me pay back every cent they invested on my sister, or worse, they won't pay for my college education.

"Since you've taken it upon yourself to control her life and parent for her, you get to fix this situation," my mom says. "Find her a job, get her a career. Fix what you've broken, Eileen."

I wince. "Okay," I whisper.

My mom points to the door. I take the cue to run. I can still hear them shouting, but it's easier to drown it out once I'm out of their bedroom. I go looking for Charlie.

She's out in the backyard, sitting on one of our swings. She's staring listlessly at the view of the mountains peaking over our fence.

"Mind if I sit here?" I ask, approaching her carefully.

Charlie nods slowly. The glazed look in her eyes fades as she turns to stare at me. I guess she was just daydreaming. She used to get high a lot in high school. I could never understand what the appeal was, but she always seemed happier during those quiet moments before she came down.

A year ago, she told me she had a bad trip and as a result, she wanted to get clean. She told me not to help her anymore because she wanted to do things on her own. Wanted to stand on her own two feet for once. I guess it worked because she stopped calling me in the middle of the night, sobbing that everyone hates her.

She grins at me sadly. It doesn't explain where she'd go when she was ditching class—or how she spent the last four months of her life.

We sit there for a while, the late spring breeze pushing us lightly as it rushes past us. The crickets keep us from falling into unbearable silence.

"What now?" she asks at some point.

I take a deep breath. If I were being honest, I'd say, "I don't know, I think we're fucked."

Neither of us have the privilege of time or uncertainty, however.

Instead I say, "We have options. You could go to another school—"

"No, Eileen," she says. "I'm never going back to school it's—it's too hard, okay?"

I nod. "There's lots of things you can try. Like so many fucking careers and businesses that don't necessarily need a degree."

She sighs. "Like what?"

"Like... a party planner?"

"You're kidding, right?"

I shrug. "You love parties, decorations, telling people what to do?"

She laughs. It helps ease the tension out of my shoulders.

Charlie scoots over, leaning her head on my shoulder. We watch the sunset together.

"Okay, weddings, bar mitzvahs, baptisms and everything you need," she says softly. "Let's try that."

37

Jason

AFTER SHE FINISHES THE STORY, I only have one thing to say, "I hate your parents so goddamn much."

Are they fucking crazy?

Where do they live? The stone age where parents are infallible and can dump their shit on their kids by proxy?

On some level they have to realize that Charlie's bullshit is their fault. Clearly, they think they're responsible enough that they have to pull Charlie out of every situation she gets herself in.

And yet too incapable that they don't help her the way she really needs it. I scrub my face. What a fucking show!

Marek's kid is fucked if this is Charlie's model of "good" parenting.

"They're not—"

"Eileen with all due respect, *please* don't end that sentence with 'that bad'," I say.

She lets out a loud sigh. "I get it, though. I fucked up Charlie's life. I'm just so tired of making up for it."

I cross the kitchen, taking her hands in mine and squeezing them.

"Eileen, I need you to listen to me very carefully," I say, eyes pleading. "If there's nothing else you ever remember about me for the rest of your life just remember this okay?"

"Okay..." she says.

"And you can't interrupt me, promise?"

"Promise, but—"

"Your parents are idiots. Wait, hear me out okay," I say, squeezing her hands gently. "You were a kid! Trying to help your sister not flunk out of school! Did she fucking cheat? Uh yeah, but that's her fault, and it was her choice to stop. Her choices aren't your fault. Your parents not having the fucking bandwidth to process their failures and treat you with the love and respect you deserve is also not your fault. You got that?"

She takes a deep breath, nodding slowly.

"Good," I say quietly. "And if anything, they should be apologizing to you. Maybe you screwed up by enabling Charlie when you were younger. But your penance fucking far outweighs your sins. That's cruel. They need to move on and so should you."

No wonder she doesn't believe in herself.

How dare they take this amazing woman for granted? I want to build a shield around her and protect her from them.

"In hindsight, I think Charlie had dyslexia and maybe ADHD," she murmurs. "I couldn't diagnose that but it makes sense. My parents wouldn't know what to look for. Lots of parents don't know and don't bother to research."

"That was on them. You did what you could."

"Fuck, my life is a mess," she says while scrubbing her face. "I wish this wedding would disappear."

"I'm afraid that isn't possible, but we *could* ditch," I propose wondering if Jossie can have a charter ready in a couple of hours.

Aruba doesn't sound bad, and it's Eileen's birthday.

"We're in the wedding party," she says with a sad smile. "Our attendance is a little mandatory."

We could go anywhere, as long as it makes you happy, I think.

I squeeze her hand. "If that's what you want."

"Uh, it's getting late," she says. "I have to get to my parents' houset o get ready for the wedding."

During the drive, she hums along to the radio in the car. I'll take it as a good enough sign. She's a fucking badass. She can survive a few hours alone with her family. We'll get through the wedding and then afterward—

I don't know what happens afterward. I guess I'll figure that out when we get there.

"Call me if you need anything," I say as I park in front of her house.

"I'll be fine," she reassures me as she opens the car door, and I wonder if she's convincing me, or herself.

"Eileen, seriously." I lean over the center console. "You don't have to do this alone. It's your birthday and your life for fuck's sake."

She gives me a sad smile, leaning over to pat my cheek. I close the gap between us, kissing her on the lips.

This kiss is less heated than what we've been doing for the last two days. It's quick, soft, and fucking domestic.

It's like coming home after a long year, or *years.*

"I'll be okay," she says. "See you later, okay?"

She gets out, slamming the door shut before I can argue.

I watch her disappear into her parents' house. "Okay."

38

Eileen

DESPITE HOW CONFIDENT and calm I tried to sound in front of Jason, I'm stressed out of my mind. There's a million ways this wedding can go wrong and only one way for it to go right. If anything's out of place, it'll be held against me. It will probably come up at every family function for the rest of my life. Maybe I should stop arriving late and just ditch them all. Now there's a happy solution.

I don't look back as I head into my parents' house. But the second the door shuts, I glance through the peephole. Jason's car stays out there for a minute before peeling out of the driveway.

I shudder as my heart skips a beat. He's a good friend, I tell myself. He isn't kidding about ditching the wedding if I want.

Too bad ditching was never an option.

I would do anything for my family. That's what families are supposed to be for—banding together in the hard times and cheering each other on in the easy times.

Family is supposed to be there when no one else will. Regardless of our flaws, they're supposed to see past that and help us pick ourselves back up—just like we'd do for them.

Jason is right. I'm loyal to a fault. I have a sense of responsibility to my family that they've never had towards me, even when things were better around here.

Charlie used to be so good, though. She's so sensitive, but she had such a kind heart. She was so empathetic.

She was a fire that could only be quenched by helping others. That's something I always admired about her. I think somewhere along the way, the person she was disappeared.

And so, I did everything in my power to get her back by assuming her life—living for her and everyone else instead of me.

I kinda feel like an idiot right now. But that's life, I guess. I can't get my sister back; I just have to live with the person she became.

Or don't. Just walk away, I imagine Jason saying.

Maybe being a good aunt will remind Charlie of everything we used to have. Someday we might heal.

"Eileen, is that you?" my mom shouts.

I wipe a tear from the corner of my eye. "Yeah, I'm here."

She comes storming into the living room. "Well, it's about time. Come on, the stylist is here and she'll need ample time to fix your hair."

There's no happy birthday hug or even an acknowledgment that today isn't just about Charlie. I open my mouth to make a sarcastic comment, but I shut it. What's the point?

Nodding, I numb myself a little. Besides getting trashed out of my mind, blocking everyone out is the only way I'm going to get through today.

It's May 27th, my twenty-seventh birthday. I wanted it to be the most amazing birthday I've ever had *and it still could be.*

I just have to survive my family.

"Eileen, finally," Charlie groans as I'm ushered into our parents' bedroom. "Tiffany can't start my hair until she finishes yours, and we're already an hour behind schedule."

"No, we're not," I say. "We have four hours until we need to leave for—"

"Actually, we're leaving in two hours now because some of my LA friends surprised me and came in for the wedding," she says. "And they want to drink before the wedding, and I want pictures with them before they're too drunk on absinthe to stand."

Joy, we have more unexpected guests.

Eileen: *Her L.A. friends decided to come.*

Jason: *On it, don't worry.*

Eileen: *Thank you. You're the best.*

Jason: *No, you are but I'll take the compliment.*

"Cool," I mutter. "Let's hurry up then."

Charlie grins. I haven't seen that excitement in her eyes in a really long time.

Despite everything, Charlie is still one of the most important people in my life. Her being happy makes all of this seem less shitty.

Her wishing me a happy birthday would make all of this worth it. Even on the ride down to the venue, I wait for that moment.

It never comes.

That's fine, I remind myself. All I have to do is survive this wedding. Whatever they do is fine. It's Charlie's big day. My mom's dream wedding.

Everything is going to be fine.

39

Eileen

Two hours before the wedding

FOUR HOURS LATER, and I'm ready to murder someone.

Holy shit, weddings are a nightmare. That's it, I'm never getting married. To quote Dr. Seuss, not here, not there. Not in a church, and never close to this bunch.

The band is fucking late. The food is too early. Marek ordered a fucking ice sculpture at the last minute because he thought that would be "romantic."

I can't find anywhere to put the damn thing that is supposed to be my sister's image... and looks nothing like her.

I swear if Charlie doesn't kill him within the next year, I'll do it myself.

Oh, and don't get me started on the flowers. Fortunately, the bouquets were fixed, and we managed with the floral decorations Charlie changed fifteen million times. I said it once and I'll say it again, peonies are beautiful.

And on the list of how things were fucked a million ways, the bridesmaids have informed me that they forgot the party favors for everyone in their hotel rooms. They are staying on the other side of Colorado Springs to save money. So, Jason had to call their hotel to get them and pay for a courier to have them sent down here.

"Fuck everyone. Let them live without their shitty party favors," I tell him.

"Normally I'd say, *that's the spirit*. But since someone said we had an *obligation* to be here, we might as well do it right," he says.

I rub my temple. "I don't think they're worth wasting your money."

Jason frowns. "Well, duh, but it's not for them."

"So, what's—"

"This nightmare is almost over," he reminds me, grabbing my hand and dusting kisses on my wrist. "You wanted a perfect wedding, so I'm going to make sure it happens."

Without thinking, I hug him tightly.

"Thank you so much," I murmur into his chest. "I don't know how I would've survived today, or any of this, without you."

He squeezes me back, kissing the top of my head. It blows me away every time this tall, muscular guy gives the gentlest hugs. He's so high energy, but he's also so *soft*.

Loving.

"Ditto, and thank *you*," he says. "This could've been the worst few weeks of my life. But it was the exact opposite."

I bury my face deeper in his chest, trying to hide my stupid blush.

"That was all you, birthday girl," he says and just his presence makes this manageable.

It's weird how this is already the best birthday I've had in years or maybe ever. It's so incredibly stressful, but I don't have to do it on my own.

The clicking of stiletto heels interrupts us.

"Your wedding is falling apart. No surprises, but I'm pitching in," Jossie says.

Jason clears his throat. "Jossie we got—"

"Darlings, let's be reasonable here," she interrupts him, lifting her finger. "You've done a wonderful job considering the cards you were dealt. But the day of the ceremony involves a lot of oversight that you don't have time for."

"You're right," I agree, grateful for her presence. "It'd be amazing if you could help, just tell me how much we need to pay—"

"Don't," Jossie puts a finger on my lips. "Think of this as a wedding present to a family friend. And part one of your birthday gifts from me."

"Part One?" My eyes get wet. "Thank you, Jossie."

She bends over to hug me. "It's my pleasure. You deserve it."

This has to be a dream. My day just got so much easier.

"Now go on," she says, shooing us away. "Go be with the bride and groom. I'll take care of the rest."

———

WE'RE ALREADY FIFTEEN MINUTES LATE FOR THE WEDDING when Charlie finally gets out of the restroom next to the bridal suite.

"Ready?" I ask anxiously, trying not to stare at my watch.

Charlie nods, "I've made the decision not to get married today."

"What?!" Mom squawks behind me.

"I think it's best that we postpone this ceremony indefinitely," Charlie says with an even tone.

"Eileen," Mom hisses. "Say something."

Great, cold feet duty. I grunt. Well, I shouldn't be complaining. This is a typical job for the Maid of Honor.

"Charlie," I say slowly. "How are you feeling?"

She crosses her arms. "I woke up at five this morning to puke. How do you think I'm doing?"

Peachy?

"That's fair," I say. "Do you need water? A snack?"

She nods. Mom and one of her friends get her to sit down in one of the chairs the bridesmaids have been occupying while I pull out her water bottle and a granola bar from my purse.

We let her eat for a minute. Once she finishes, I kneel down in front of her.

I take a long deep breath and ask her, "Okay, how are you now?"

"Better," she says drinking her water. "But I'm still not getting married."

I swear, if I wasn't looking at her, I'd guess a five year-old had spoken just about now.

Holy fuck. "Can we talk about it? Why don't you want to get married?"

She shrugs, still eating. "It's just so fucking stupid. Getting married because we're having a kid together. What was I thinking?"

Finally, I think. Why couldn't she have figured this out two fucking weeks ago.

"Let me get this straight then. We're calling off the wedding," I confirm, more like calling her bluff because this sounds like a last-minute temper tantrum.

Charlie shakes her head. "Just postponing it."

What the fuck does this mean? Why does she have to pull this bullshit today of all days?

Right, because it's Charlie.

"Charlotte, that's—"

"Mom, please," I snap. "Give her a minute."

My mom fumes, but I don't give a fuck. It's not actually her call.

"So, you don't want to marry Marek at all?" I ask.

"That's not what I said," Charlie says aggravated.

"You said we should 'cancel indefinitely,'" I repeat her words.

"Well at least until the baby comes," she says.

I take a deep breath. "Do you love him?"

"Yes," she says.

"Do you want to spend the rest of your life with him?"

"Yes," she says earnestly.

Surprising, but okay. That's reassuring to know.

"So, what's the problem?"

She starts crying, "All of my friends are wasted, and I can't drink with them."

I sigh. Okay, this is manageable. She's just being a brat.

"Charlie, it's one day. You can drink with them some other time, when you don't have a baby to think about," I say. "And wouldn't it be nice to remember your whole wedding day, instead of how hungover you were afterward or how pretty the pictures are?"

She shrugs. "It's not the same."

"I get that—"

"No offence, Eileen, but what would you know about parties or having fun?"

I lean back and look at her. She seriously doesn't know me, does she? What does she think I do with my life?

I take a deep breath. "That's not the point, Charlie. We're talking about you giving up on your big day. You've worked so hard—"

"Shut up, shut up!" She screams at me. "You're such a fucking kill joy. You just hate me."

I can't believe I have to say this but— "I don't hate you. You're my sister. I love—"

"You're just a bitter, heinous bitch who hates everything and wouldn't do fucking shit for me if I were on the ground bleeding," she says.

"Do you hear yourself?" I say, my composure breaking. "I get it, you're stressed. It's been a long day. If it'd make you happy, we can postpone but—"

"You're not listening!" She shouts. "You fucking whore! I hate you."

I swallow and cross my arms. "Then say it again. What am I not listening to?"

"This wedding is stupid, and I deserve to get drunk." Charlie says. "Cancel it right now. Jason will just pay for the next one."

"Okay fi—" I cut myself off.

Normally, I would just listen to her. Let it go. Move the fuck on because it doesn't matter.

Only it does. It so fucking matters.

"No," I say evenly. "We're not cancelling the wedding."

"What?" Charlie says.

"You're going to finish that water, get up, and go get married," I instruct her. "Everything will run smoothly from this point forward."

Charlie goes red. "That's not what—"

"I don't care what you said—or think you want," I tell her. "You know, you've pulled a lot of stupid stunts in your life. But this is really up there."

"Eileen, be reasonable," Mom says. "If she doesn't want to get married—"

I toss my hands up in the air. Is she kidding me? It's *not* okay to cancel. Does she just like to fuck with me?

"Oh no, if she didn't want to get married, I'd support that," I say. "Planning this wedding has been a nightmare my ungrateful family shoved on me."

Charlie growls. "No one asked for your help!"

"Really?" I say incredulously tossing the wedding journal at her feet. "'Eileen, use the Pinterest board. Eileen, get the roses. No, I want daisies. No, Eileen I hate daisies, what are you? A stupid bitch?'"

I find myself laughing, as a tear rolls down my cheek. "You used to be my hero, you know? I would do anything for the Charlie who would fight bullies for me and told me I could be an artist if I wanted."

Shaking my head, I continue. "But now you're selfish, ungrateful, and I can't take it anymore."

"Eileen," my mother says in a threatening tone. "This isn't the time—"

"It's never the right time, Mother," I snap. "I'm sick of making up for your neglection toward Charlie and making me pay for it."

I dust off my dress. I sigh as Charlie glares at me. Her lip starts to wobble as if that's going to assuage my anger.

"If you hate me, I have no problem with never seeing you again after today," I say simply. "But Jason, myself, and a shit ton of your friends and family bent over backward to make today happen for you. Something our mother didn't even offer to help with."

"And it had to be today of all days." I snort.

I look between my sister and mother. Charlie starts sobbing quietly while my mother has the decency to blush. I didn't expect her to remember. As angry as I am, I really pity them.

"You ruined my graduation day," I say firmly. "You stole my fucking birthday. You're not allowed to ruin this beautiful wedding. So get over your stupid bullshit. You can have a belated bachelorette party next year. I'm sure Marek would love that."

"Sweetheart," my mom says, trying to reach out to me.

I wave her off. "I don't care."

I offer Charlie a hand. Hesitantly, she takes it.

"Come on, Charlie," I say with a sad smirk. "Let's get you hitched."

40

Jason

I NEED about two more cups of coffee and a shot of something hard to deal with this ceremony. We're already twenty minutes late.

Jackson and Alex are standing in as groomsmen. My parents couldn't make it. Their flight got delayed, and they are stuck in New York. My sisters are also here. Because even when Mar is a pain in the ass, we love him. He's like a brother.

"The ceremony hasn't started," Jack mumbles under his breath.

"I called it," Alex mutters. "You owe me something."

I roll my eyes and shake my head. I'm not thrilled about being close to an altar waiting for a fucking bride. Do they have to behave this way? I check my phone, but there're no texts from Eileen. If Charlie had run away, she'd have told me.

But, after the ten-minute mark, I volunteer to go looking for the bride. If she flakes, I'd prefer to find out sooner rather than later.

I have to walk around half of the venue to get to the bridal suite. As I approach, everything starts to make a lot more sense.

I can already hear Charlie pitching a fit, which is to be expected honestly.

What I don't expect is Eileen's voice, shouting right back.

"—Jason, myself, and a shit ton of your friends and family bent over backward to make today happen for you. Something your mother didn't even offer to help with.," Eileen says.

True. I'm surprised she's pointing it out though.

"You ruined my graduation day," she continues.

Wow, we're going there.

I stop in front of the door—no use interrupting when Eileen's finally telling them what's up. I lean against the door frame, impressed as fuck.

"Sweetheart—" her mom says.

I roll my eyes.

"I don't care," Eileen yells, and I wonder if the wedding guests can hear the throw down.

Who cares? The smile on my face is so broad it hurts. That's *my Eileen*, tough and capable.

She deserves to know her worth. What's reasonable to ask of her, and when she deserves care and support.

It feels like she knows it for once.

When the door swings open, Eileen is pulling Charlie through the threshold.

"Everything alright here?" I ask cautiously.

Eileen huffs, tucking a piece of hair behind her ear. "Yeah, I think so."

I look at Charlie, who's kind of a wreck around her eyes. Good thing Jossie has shit to touch her face up before the reception.

"You ready to get married?" I ask Charlie.

She sniffles, looking at Eileen who refuses to meet her gaze.

"Yeah," Charlie says. "I'm ready."

———

THE WEDDING FINALLY GETS UNDERWAY. A HARPIST BEGINS

playing softly in the corner. All the decorations and people are set, and the wedding party goes down the aisle seamlessly.

Then, it's Eileen and me walking down side by side.

"Nervous?" I whisper and link her pinky with mine.

"Not anymore," she says with a smirk.

"You're a fucking badass," I say. "You should be proud of yourself."

"Takes one to know one," she says.

Just as we part at the front of the room, I squeeze her hand and walk to my side.

It's sort of a Catholic ceremony. The minister is Lutheran. Which, Eileen explained to me is... different. Mainly he added more readings, but not so many that it's as long as Eileen's grandparents expected it to be.

Which, thank God, because I don't know what we'd do if they don't approve since I'm not helping, or paying, for another wedding.

"And now," the minister says at some point. "The bride and groom have elected to recite their own vows."

My eyes catch Eileen's as she hands Charlie a piece of paper. I swallow thickly. This... this could be good. Unless Eileen didn't do what we agreed on.

———

3 days ago

I BANG MY HEAD AGAINST MY COFFEE TABLE. "THEY'VE GOT TO be fucking kidding me."

"I wish," Eileen says, lying on my area rug. Max is just right beside her, belly up sleeping.

She's hiding her eyes under one of her checklists. It's kinda cute.

"There was a list, and that list had a sublist," she mutters. "I gave her three things to do. Tell me who your bridesmaids are, pick your wedding dress, and write your wedding vows."

"I'd say two out of three ain't bad, but she barely did one of those," I joke.

She groans. "How the fuck do we write vows for someone else's wedding?"

We sit there in silence for a while. How in-fucking-deed. This is way beyond the job description.

Then again, we could get creative with this.

I nudge her shoulder with my foot. "Hey, Eileen."

"What?"

"What if we act while we write these?"

She sits up, blinking at me. "I gotta be honest, that's the weirdest thing I've ever heard you say, and I won't pretend it made any sense."

"What if... we pretend we're in love with someone or something. Talk about love, embellish it a little bit. Let them edit it last minute and boom, corny vows that no one will ever remember anyway."

"I could live with that," she says.

She pulls out a notebook from her bag, handing it to me with a pen. "Let's try to go for one page, front and back."

I stare at my paper for a while, waiting for the muse to strike me.

"Uh, I know I suggested this but... how do we actually do this?" I ask.

Eileen looks up from the paper she's been furiously scribbling on for a while.

"I don't know," she says with a shrug.

"What? You've been writing like a maniac for—" I check the clock on the wall. "Twenty minutes."

"Yeah, kind of," she mutters.

What does she have there, a three-page essay on coffee?

"Let me see," I request.

She clutches her notebook close to her chest. "No, that's okay."

"Come on, Eileen," I say, reaching over. "Show me."

"It's not done yet!"

She scoots away from me. I get on the ground for a better angle.

"It can't be that bad!" I say, making a grab for her notebook.

We tug back and forth a little bit. But finally, I get the upper hand.

Yanking it just hard enough to get it into my hands—

—Which causes Eileen to land on top of me.

"Finally—"

Her paper is a drawing of *me*.

"Are you kidding?" I ask pretending to be upset but actually amused. "You've been drawing?"

"I was stuck! What do I know about love?"

I shrug, inspecting her drawing more closely. It's a little cartoon-ish, but so accurate. She's got all these great details of my hair, my eyes, my nose—

"I don't have this many freckles," I say, pointing to the drawing.

She looks between me and the paper, shrugging.

"They look cute on you," she says.

Her eyes, those are cute, I think distractedly. Her eyes and her voice, plus the way she keeps tucking a pen behind her ear and then immediately forgets where it is. The way her hands flit across a page as she draws is super cute.

It's strange the things people can find beautiful in the odd and mundane.

"Why don't we start over? Together," I suggest.

Eileen nods. "You've been engaged before. What do you know about love?"

I laugh. "Not as much as I thought I did when I first proposed but —listen, love is complicated, and it changes. It changes all the time. What matters the most is that you care about someone or something else a whole fucking lot and are willing to put the work in to figure things out."

"Like compromising," she surmises.

"Sure, but it's only a compromise if everyone's happy and comfortable with the changes. If couples just meet somewhere in the middle for the sake of saying they tried, it's kinda bullshit and no one's happy."

She nods, taking down some notes.

Then she looks at me a strangely, kind of like with all these questions but also with secrets.

"Okay," she says after a long silence. "But we need to write about big sweeping love that makes people cry at a wedding. How do we do that?"

I shrug. "It's not about them. Cool if they get emotional, but it's not about what other people think. It's about seeing this person in front of you and thinking—"

I glance at her bright, inquisitive eyes.

I clear my throat. "Thinking wow, this person inspires me. This person makes me feel good shit about myself, and I want them to feel that all the time. I wanna be around them for as long as they can stand me."

"Alright," Eileen says. "I think I can figure something out."

———

Now

"Marek," Charlie says, reading the paper Eileen handed to her.

"I can't begin to tell you how much this day has made me feel. Excited, nervous, joyful, hopeful, and a little sad. Sad because every day you're in my life is the best day of my life. I just cannot believe it took us so long to find each other.

"There are so many things I want to say to you, but I'm scared that if I get them all down, we could be here a while."

The crowd laughs.

"But I will say this," Charlie says. "You are so witty, lively, and charming. You are a bright light in a very dark world that I would do anything to protect. You're so free-spirited yet so measured. I promise to never discourage your smile or ambitions."

Marek's the least ambitious person I know—

Oh right, Eileen wrote this.

I tilt my head to get a better look at her. Her eyes catch mine, almost instantly looking away as her cheeks go red.

"You're more than the tangible things, and you're so much more than the sum of your parts. You see something in me that I can only hope I live up to. You cherish the little things in a way I'm only starting to learn. I want to spend the rest of our lives learning from each other.

"I want each moment to be as breathtaking, exhilarating, and entertaining as the last. I want to see the world through your eyes because they hold the kindest mind and most profound soul I've ever known."

Wait a minute. Eileen said I'm the kindest person she's ever met. Shit, she wrote about me?

She wrote what she thinks about me? I'm her inspiration for wedding vows.

A breath gets lodged in my throat and I realize, this is the most important wedding I've ever been to.

"You're an entire universe of love, hope, loss, and perseverance. I know the big things scare you sometimes. I know you aren't sure of yourself. But I'm here to say that if I could be even a portion as good and wonderful as you've been in our time together—I'd be the happiest, most fulfilled person on the planet."

Charlie slows, something in her eye. "Because anything, or anyone, as good as you is truly amazing. Every day we're together, I feel myself growing into the person who supports you better, and makes you laugh harder. You're a love song I never want to stop playing, and a dream I never want to wake up from.

"With that in mind, I promise to take the new and the unexpected in stride. To treat you with the patience and respect you deserve," Charlie says. "I promise to always take you seriously and respect the things you value. I vow to give you back the comfort, confidence, and love you've given me tenfold. I vow to be your partner-in-crime and your best friend. I vow, through good times and bad to be by your side. I love you and will gladly spend the rest of my life proving that."

When Charlie finishes, she bites her lip and laughs.

She says, "I love you, baby," to Marek.

Eileen's wiping something out of her eyes.

My heart thunders inside my chest. She really meant it—all of it. She wants me. She *loves* me. We could have everything, and that would make her happy.

Fuck, life is so confusing, and love is just a fucking curveball we're thrown. I sigh. I think I'm less scared than I used to be.

Love is scary as fuck, but what I feel for Eileen isn't. It's exciting. It's the best fucking adventure of my entire life.

She finally looks up as Marek clears his throat. I flash her a reassuring smile. Pretty sure it wobbles a little. My gaze is steady and that's what matters.

I nod, pointing my head to Marek. I'm trying to tell her "Listen up, this one's dedicated to you" without using my own voice. Just the words I wrote for my cousin's vows.

"Charlie, Charlotte, Charlie Bear," Marek says.

Ad libbing, huh? I definitely didn't tell him he could do that. It's fine, I remind myself as long as he doesn't fuck up my speech.

"Every day that I get to wake up and see you, talk to you, and feel you is the best day of my life," Marek says.

"Every time I turn around and don't see you, I get turned around because you're my compass—my guiding light. You give me so much, and you ask for so little."

Eileen bites back a smile. She knows that can't be about Charlie, *good*.

"You see the very best in me. Sometimes that scares me because I've never seen someone so amazing have so much optimism for other people. I want to spend every moment we have reminding you of all the things you've already given to me—the laughs, the love, the support, and the happiness that comes with being by your side.

"I want to be the person that reminds you to take a break, to be more loving to yourself because you're so deserving of love. You're so much braver, kinder, and tenacious than you give yourself credit for—I vow to spend the rest of my life reminding you of that."

Marek pauses. "I vow to make every day we get together as incredible as you. I vow to remind you whenever possible that you're—

Beautiful, intelligent, hilarious, vivacious, creative, and warm-hearted, I mouth to Eileen.

"And you deserve all the love you bring to this world," Marek says.

Eileen's lip wobbles. I would give anything to be able to cross this aisle and kiss her right now.

"I vow to listen, speak clearly, and be as patient as you need me to be," Marek smirks. "Within reason, of course."

Everyone, minus Eileen, laughs.

She smirks at me. Yeah, that was me being serious—I know my limitations.

I'm impatient as fuck.

"But I'll always try for you," Marek says. "I vow to never give up. Even when things get hard. You're the Hall to my Oats, the Simon to my Garfunkel. You're my partner-in-crime, and my wildest dreams come true.

"I vow to spend every day cherishing everything you are and everything you bring to me. I love you more than life itself."

The minister asks for the rings. One of Eileen's cousins walks toward them holding the pillow. Charlie and Marek fidget putting them on and once they are done, the minister pronounces them husband and wife.

And while all this happens, my eyes are only for Eileen.

My beautiful woman. If she'll take me.

41

Eileen

The Reception

AFTER THE NUPTIALS, I'm on edge as we walk down the aisle.

Jason whispers, "On my signal, follow me. We're running away."

As soon as we're out of eyesight from the wedding guests, I take off my heels, Jason loosens his tie, and we make a break for it. We run as fast as we can, as far away from the rest of the wedding as we can.

The sun hasn't started setting yet, but the sprinklers are already going on the golf course. The sky's still so beautiful and bright as the wet grass nips my feet and Jason tries (poorly) to shield us from blasts of water.

I'm laughing so hard I can barely catch my breath. His hand doesn't let go of mine the entire way. It feels so warm, protective... it feels so *right* in mine.

"Where are we going?!" I shout at one point around the 16th hole.

"Anywhere we want!" He shouts back.

I slow down. "You had no real escape plan, did you?"

He stops running, panting heavily. "Well—I don't know; it seemed right in the moment?"

We stare at each other for a second. The laughter slips out of us easily, like it always does.

Except this time, it ends with Jason wrapping his arms around my waist as he leans in to kiss me.

He kisses like it's the first, last, and best kiss all combined. It's like getting lost in a supernova of emotions.

Jason pulls me in closer, anchoring me against him as we deepen the kiss.

Fuck, we really need to talk about what happened back there during the ceremony.

"We can't have sex on the golf course," I say.

"I could buy the golf course," he rasps. "Then it wouldn't matter."

"Don't," I say. "There are thousands of other places you can buy that we could have sex on."

He chuckles. "Yeah? You mean that?"

I lick my lips, shuddering. He can be so distracting with his... everything.

Focus, this is important, I remind myself.

"Why don't you ask me what you really want to know?" I whisper. "Don't you think you deserve good things too?"

His lips twitch. He almost smiles. He's so fucking hesitant.

I get it, but it takes two to tango. He has to be brave too.

"Do we have to be friends that hook up?" He asks softly.

I kiss his lips quickly. "What kind of friends do you think we should be instead? The kind that live together?"

"Maybe someday," he says cupping my face and kissing my nose. "We could also be the kind of friends who love each other very fucking much, and who say that a lot while they go on adventures together—"

"Kinda like dates?"

"Not only dates," He says.

"And then what?" I ask. "Be the kind of friends who don't want to look for another friend ever again because their current friend is more than they could've ever asked for?"

He kisses me again, and again, and again.

I get lost in the way his kisses say the same thing he whispered as we walked out of the wedding, arm in arm.

I love you. I love you. I. Love. *You.*

This man is ridiculous, loud, soft, energetic, serious, and everything in between. Putting myself out there is hard. I still feel like I'm dreaming because I don't get the guy or the happy endings. I get a flurry of dead ends and half-assed apologies that hardly ever come.

Being vulnerable is so fucking hard. It's such a risk to put my real self in front of someone else and say, "Here I am, warts and all, accept or reject what I have to offer." It's crazy scary and something I've never wanted to do before.

For Jason, though, it doesn't feel crazy. It feels like floating on a cloud, falling gently to somewhere safe to land. Somewhere safe that I've been searching for my entire life.

Being vulnerable for Jason isn't easy, not by a long shot. But thinking about what he said in those vows—

I vow to spend every day cherishing everything you are and everything you bring to me—

It makes me realize that love, being intimate and vulnerable, isn't about being confident enough to conquer the world. It's about being patient, listening, and learning how to grow into the people we need to be, *together.*

For him, I would try anything. I can't imagine who I'd be if he hadn't... happened upon me.

If he hadn't happened to me, really.

"Yeah," I say when we stop kissing. "I don't want to hook up just for the weekend. I'm yours, Jason Spearman, for as long as you'll have me."

He flashes me an ear-splitting grin. He kisses me on the head.

"Good. You already stole my heart, Eileen McBean," Jason says. "At this point, I'm not sure you'll ever give it back, and I can't live without it. Without you."

I laugh, leaning in for another kiss.

Getting drenched in more sprinkler water feels poetic. Perfect.

———

EVENTUALLY, WE MAKE OUR WAY BACK TO THE WEDDING. WE missed the after-ceremony pictures, but they got us in the pre-ceremony pictures, so it'll be fine.

Leave it to Charlie to do multiple shoots during her wedding. I'm sure her friends are all jumping at the chance to snap their own pictures for social media.

Dinner goes off without a hitch. So do the speeches. A few days ago, Charlie asked if Jason and I would mind giving our speech time to other people in the wedding party who are from out of town.

Apparently, distance means not seeing them as often so it's more important that they speak than the Maid of Honor and Best Man.

Fast forward to the reception and I couldn't be happier with that decision. I don't have a nice thing to say to Charlie right now. But regardless of how I feel, she deserves a good wedding reception.

Dancing starts, so does the mischievous look on Jason's face. When the father-daughter dance is over, and the ballroom opens for general dancing, he leans over the table.

"Would you mind if I have this dance?" he asks, offering me his hand.

I take it without hesitation. "I'd be insulted if you didn't."

The band we chose is perfect. They take a few requests as we dance around the ballroom.

At some point, my brother, Sam, cuts in.

"You mind if I dance with my sister, bro?" He asks Jason.

Jason looks at me, I shrug and nod.

Sam's never been a part of the problem.

"I'm grabbing something from the bar," he says. "Want anything?"

"See if they have something seasonal," I call out as he walks away.

Sam's never been one for dancing. I should admit he's not terrible at it.

"So, I heard you told Mom and Charlie off," Sam says.

I sigh. "Yeah, something like that."

"That's pretty badass," he says.

"Yeah? You think so?"

"Definitely," he says. "It's about time someone told them what's up. I've still got a few months left of living there so fuck if I could."

Thinking about who we were as kids, life wasn't fair to Sam either. Sure, he was their only son, so Dad would jump hoops for him when he had the time. But he was never as important as Charlie. It sucked for me, but I escaped for a few years during undergrad.

How did he survive a household with my parents, Charlie, and no buffer?

"I'm sorry we were never close," I say.

"Don't sweat it, Elie," Sam says. "Wasn't your job to fix us. Shouldn't be your job now."

"Well, as of today, I officially quit," I say.

He laughs and then spins me. "Good."

It's funny how long we've gone without really talking about the shit we've lived through or the way Mom and Dad are. I guess it's easy to lose perspective when it feels like a competition for love and attention.

"I can't believe you pulled this off," Sam says.

"Can't you? I have three notebooks in my giant mom bag," I say.

"Fine, I believe it," he says as he looks around the room. "Would've been nicer if we could've gone to Aruba."

"Yeah," I say, exhaling deeply.

"Sorry about your birthday, sis," he says.

"It is what it is," I say.

"Don't say that," Charlie's voice appears out of nowhere.

Sam and I turn around. Charlie's standing there awkwardly, clasping her hands tight.

"Mind if I cut in?" Charlie asks.

Sam shrugs. "Your funeral."

I roll my eyes. "Sam, go find Jossie. I'm sure there's something she can find for you to do."

Completely misinterpreting things like I knew he would, he pats me on the shoulder. "Later."

Charlie steps forward. "Uh, who leads?"

I roll my eyes. "Come here, I will."

We dance slowly. It's kind of awkward considering the day we've had.

"Happy Birthday," Charlie says.

"Uh huh," I say.

"Elie, listen—" She cuts herself off.

"I'm listening," I say.

"This is the part where I'd normally be shouting at someone," she says.

I nod. "You should talk to a professional, not me, about why you do that."

She blushes. "You're probably right."

"I know," I say, keeping shit light. "So, what do you want?"

"I'm sorry," she says. "I'm sorry I shoved the wedding on you. I'm sorry I was fucking bridezilla every step of the way. And for a long time before it. This pregnancy—"

"Don't blame your kid for shit that's not their fault," I say. "Learn from Mom and Dad's mistakes and hold yourself accountable like an adult."

She sighs. "I've been a bitch. I've been a bitch for a really long time. And before I was a bitch, I was a fucking mess—"

"Yeah, but you tried when you were a mess," I argue as we keep dancing. "And you weren't a mess. You were just a kid who needed special accommodations in school that you never got. And like, not having that support means you learned to cope with hard shit and your emotions through maladaptive habits like binge drinking and running away at the first sign of trouble."

"Where's the 'but,'" she says.

I groan, spinning her. "But you're almost in your thirties, you can't hold down a fucking job, and you have a kid who deserves goddamn better. Pull it together, stop dicking around."

She nods. "Thanks, I needed to hear that."

I don't answer.

"Is there some way I can make this up to you?"

I take a deep breath. As much as I'd love for Charlie to go back in time, not ruin her college career, and work on herself so my parents would get off my neck—there's no changing the past. What's done is done.

The best she can do for anyone is to be better for herself and then worry about fixing shit with other people.

"I don't want you to try to make up for Mom and Dad's mistakes," I say. "I spent so many years doing that. It doesn't go anywhere, and I think I wound up resenting myself for trying.

"What you can do is go to therapy. Work on yourself because you wanna grow in some aspect. Do it for you and your kid, no one else."

"And then what?" Charlie asks.

"And then come visit me some time," I say. "I don't like the person who rushed a last-minute wedding. But I do miss my sister. She was pretty amazing if I remember correctly."

Charlie hugs me tightly. I feel something wet fall onto my shoulder.

"With all due respect, you're wrong, Eileen," She says. "Because you've clearly never met *my* sister. She's the most amazing person in the world."

Something wet slides down my face.

"Happy Birthday, sis," Charlie says.

I was right. It does make everything worth it.

42

Jason

IF I LOOK BACK at the last ten years of my life, nothing of what I've done has prepared me for this. But there's no logic when it comes to Eileen. She just makes me want to be *me*.

Not the guy who sleeps his way around avoiding entanglements, but the one I've been hiding for so long. This woman awakes my body, my soul, and my heart beats again when she's around.

After that kiss, my body is still buzzing. I feel alive. For the first time in a long time, I want to live in the moment. I'm still savoring the taste of her lips.

"Are you sure about this?" I ask as we walk toward the suite I got us.

She presses her hands to my chest. Her green cat eyes brighten. "Unless you think you can't handle it," she says jokingly.

I reach for her hair, threading a hand through her bouncy, soft curls. "I want you so bad." I press my lips on her ear.

She shivers, gripping the hem of my shirt in two fists. "Let me feel your lips along my skin."

With that, I crush my lips to hers. I kiss her softly, slowly, tasting her lips as if this was the first time. I push my tongue into her mouth, and she lets me in easily. Her tongue swirling along with mine. They are like two long lost lovers who finally meet after a long separation.

This isn't the first time Eileen feels familiar, fitting. I find comfort in her presence, as much as excitement and joy. A happiness I want to consume. So, I kiss her hard, and she kisses me back with the same intensity. As if we can't get enough of each other. Her lips become a flame igniting every cell of my body, burning me from the inside out.

"Hook your legs around my waist," I order. "If we do this, we have to be in bed."

I'm throbbing with desire, but I want to make this good for her. As we enter the suite's bedroom and I set her on the floor, she runs her hands over the buttons of my shirt, snapping them open easily. Once she's done, she spreads open the fabric. Her fingers touch my bare skin, searing it with lust and need.

Before she can continue, I unzip her dress, dropping it to the floor and exposing her olive skin and a pretty blue lace bra covering her beautiful tits. They are big, luscious, and I want to suck on them all night.

Her body is fucking fantastic, just like her. I can't wait to trace every inch of it with my lips and my tongue. I don't wait to make my wish a reality and start at her collarbone, sucking her sensitive skin.

Eileen moans as my mouth devours her. She trembles as my fingers slide up and down her torso. Without fumbling, she yanks my belt open, undoes my button, and unzips my zipper.

My straining cock pushes at the front of my boxer briefs. I shiver as she traces my erection with her long finger. I take her hand. "Don't do that or this will be over too soon."

I need to lose myself inside of her. Feel her body grinding against mine.

Our eyes meet as I lower myself, peeling off her matching panties. She's a fucking goddess, and I want to worship her all night long.

"I need you," she says breathlessly.

"Tell me, what do you need?"

She grabs my erection. Her touch shoots sparks through my spine all the way up my body. Her hand rubs my length. It's so fucking good I'm about to come.

But that's not enough, she drops to her knees, lowers my boxers and my shaft springs free, almost touching her beautiful lips. My cock pulses against her palm as she skims her hand upward, barely touch the head, but close enough to make my knees tremble with desire.

Oh, fuck. I've never been so turned on in my life. Our gazes lock as her mouth opens wide. Then it closes. With a smile on her face, she kisses the tip making me shiver.

"You're a tease."

She licks her lips before she runs her tongue through my length and under my balls. I let out a loud a groan when she sucks my sacks.

"It'll be my turn to torture you soon," I warn her closing my eyes.

That's when I feel her mouth swallowing me—taking me all the way down her throat. Shards of pleasure threaten to shoot every way as she sucks me while she plays with my balls.

My fingers twist in her hair as she takes me harder and deeper. My muscles tense as I'm losing control, and as much as I'm loving this mind fucking blow job, I'm not ready to come.

"As much as I love your mouth, I need to taste you," I groan and let out a hitched breath.

I pull back. My cock popping free of her mouth. "We need to stop, or I won't last. I want to make this good for you too.

"Come to bed with me," I insist, pulling her to me and slowly setting her on the bed.

Her heavy eyes stare at me, hungry and needy. I sit right next to her and lean forward, running the tip of my tongue over one of her nipples still covered by lace and satin. I hurry to unfasten her bra, releasing a pair of perfect, round globes. Reminding me they are more beautiful than my imagination does justice.

As I watch her, I don't know where to start to make this good for her. There are so many things I want to do with her, to show her. I breathe through the sudden urge that's overcoming me. Since when do I care this much about my technique? It's just sex.

For a moment I think, what am I doing? But I turn off my brain and focus on the now, kissing my way down her body. I part her thighs as wide as I can. My hands trail up her silky bare legs, starting at her ankles and making my way up her shapely calves. I gently kiss her behind her knees.

"Talking about teasing," she moans.

I smirk and kiss her outer thighs, getting closer to the apex but avoiding it.

"Jason," she says my name frustrated.

"Everything okay there?" I tease. "Is there something you'd like to request?"

It takes every shred of my willpower not to eat her. I don't want her to beg, but to ask for what she really wants. Not to just wait for someone to serve her what's left over.

"Just say the word, and it's yours," I say but continue stroking her legs with my hands and tracing the outline of her sex with my mouth, teasing her and not giving her what I know she desperately wants.

"Spearman!" she protests with a moan.

"That's not what you want, beautiful."

"You know what I want," she groans when I place a kiss so close to her swollen clit. I'm so close, I can taste her.

"Be bold, Eileen. Ask for what you want, what you deserve," I insist.

"I want your mouth on me," she speaks loudly.

"Your wish is my command, my lady," I say

I look into her soulful green eyes as my tongue flicks against her clit. She closes her eyes, arching her back as I lick one long stroke and bury my entire face between my legs. She quivers and tightens as my mouth feasts on her. Devours her. I alternate between sucking her sensitive bud, pushing my tongue inside her along with my fingers, and just nibbling her while I get turned on by the sound of her pleasure.

"Jason," she moans, and I growl, pushing further, licking faster.

Her body begins to tremble, her inside walls throbbing around my fingers. She yanks my hair, moaning as she thrashes against the bed. Her legs close on my head as she whimpers.

I rise and grab a condom from my nightstand. After rolling it down my length, I position myself on top of her. I grab my shaft, placing it softly at her entrance and look into her sweet eyes. "Are you sure about this?"

"Please," is all she says before I slip my tip inside her.

I sink in inch by inch. I groan, lost inside her eyes and press deeper. She thrusts her hips against mine until I'm all the way inside her. She feels so good. *So goddamned right.* Her hands cling to my shoulders as I begin to move. Her legs hook around my waist. We begin slowly but in seconds, we find our own rhythm, which is intense, fast, urgent—as if we can't get enough of each other.

Wrapping my arms around her, I kiss her shoulder as I rock deeper into her body. Her body tenses and then starts to quake beneath me. Small pulses squeeze my cock as she moans. My back stiffens, my balls tighten, and a quake takes over my body while I release the pent-up energy inside me.

"I love you," I whisper as I start coming down from the high. "Forever."

43

Jason

One week after the wedding

THE SOFT MELODY of a piano starts playing. It sounds like a Billy Joel cover, maybe a little in reverse. A voice begins to accompany the piano. She sounds gorgeous. Her voice wraps me in a warm embrace, like a lover I never knew I needed.

Instead of dancing like a soulless chump, desperate for one more round of applause, I search for her voice.

Wading across the stage with a simmering spotlight on me is hard, but I manage.

The piano gets to an accelerando, and I run out of shits to give. I belt out a melody of being so close yet so far—a melody to match her subtle vibrato.

She sounds like an angel waiting to take me home.

I find her lying on top of a grand piano. It's Eileen. She's in a black dress that hugs her all the way down. Her hair is curled like something out of a noir flick.

She belts into a microphone before sitting up.

232 • CLAUDIA BURGOA

"Hey, hot stuff," she says, beckoning me closer. "What took you so long?"

"I literally have no idea," I murmur.

"Come on, Jason," she says playfully. "You know this part."

I harmonize with her as I help her down from the piano. We dance slowly in circles as we sing. Not to the audience, not to anyone else. Just to each other.

My alarm goes off a little later than ass o'clock in the morning, as it always does on Sundays. I groan, stretching as I realize how fucking trapped I am in someone's hug.

I look over my shoulder, grinning when I see her head buried against my back. "Hey beautiful," I murmur.

Eileen hugs me tighter. "It's Sunday, so shush."

I chuckle, rolling over to hold her better. She hums, settling her head into the crook of my neck.

"You know... ass o'clock could be literal if we wanted it to be," I suggest. "That's one place we haven't explore yet."

She swats me lightly. "I'd rather have coffee first."

I chuckle, squeezing her tighter. "We could make arrangements for that."

She grumbles under her breath, but she kisses my neck so damn lovingly.

We get up ten minutes later, trudging into the kitchen together while I pour the coffee and she turns on the news.

"Hey, they're passing some new legislation in the state house about sales taxes," she says.

"Well, turn it the fuck up," I say enthusiastically. "Fuck yeah, let's start our morning with a party."

She laughs like a million bucks, like the sun floating around the moon, singing praises of its love.

"Come on, *Jason*," Eileen says jokingly. "Let's cuddle."

"Hey, that's my thing," I say, even though my heart fucking stutters with how perfectly she slips into my life.

We watch the news wrapped around each other, slowly sipping coffee as we quietly murmur about local events.

Yeah, this is how I want to spend every morning.

———

"ARE YOU SURE?" EILEEN SAYS A COUPLE OF HOURS LATER AS WE stand awkwardly on the most cutesy cat themed welcome mat I've ever seen.

"Sure, why not?" I ask.

"Doesn't it seem a little... soon?"

I frown. "Does it feel too soon?"

Eileen shrugs. "I guess not. I just—I'm not intruding, right? I don't want to be a nuisance—"

"Eileen, my light, my love, my precious shot of espresso," I say. "If anything, I'm the nuisance. You're more than welcome here and honestly, they're fucking thrilled."

She takes a deep breath, nodding confidently. There's my Eileen.

I knock on the door. It only takes a second for it to fly open.

"You were right behind the door, weren't you?" I say.

"Hush," Emmeline glares.

"That's—"

"No, Jason," Eileen says. "It's sweet. You'd pull that stunt any day."

Emmeline has the audacity to giggle at my expense. "See? You found a good woman here, Jase."

I say, "Don't call me that," at the same time that Eileen says, "Please don't call him that."

Emmeline rolls her eyes. "Okay, lovebirds. Anyway, come on in! And welcome, Eileen, to Sunday Brunch."

When we step in, I suck in a breath. My parents and Alex are here too.

"Where are the girls?" I ask looking around.

"Emmeline thought it'd be best if we eased Eileen into the family," Mom says as she steps closer giving me a kiss and a hug then hugging my girl. "It's so nice to meet you, dear."

I look over at Em and mouth, *thank you.*

She shrugs as if it's nothing, but I know it is. And maybe I should stop being so harsh to her when she's always so supportive.

"Everyone, the food is on the table, but you guys can eat anywhere," Em announces, and then she also hugs Eileen and says, "Welcome to the family."

Epilogue

The Next Year ...

JASON

"You want one of those, love?" I ask Eileen as she holds Caroline, one of Jack's twin daughters.

They are only a few hours old but already loved by all their uncles. Mom and Dad are over the moon. Emmeline is feeding Marianne. Mom would be holding her hostage if that wasn't the case.

"Not yet," Eileen answers kissing Caroline's forehead. "We have a lot on our plates, don't you think?"

I smile and nod.

Last September, we opened a therapeutic practice that combines everything she's always dreamt of—helping children and adults with special needs who only have to pay according to their income.

The clinic keeps me busy, and helping others is a great change of pace from what I used to do before.

"I love their names," Eileen says when Jack takes his sweet little girl from her. "But how did you guys come up with them."

Jack glances at Em who smiles at him. They don't answer, but I'm sure there's a story behind them.

I get it. There are stories worth telling and others worth living. Eileen and I share some of the pictures we take during our trips but keep the stories behind them to ourselves.

We lived them for us.

Life isn't exactly what I dreamt when I became an adult. It's actually better. Unconventional at times, but perfect for us.

Eileen and I are made for each other. We have our disagreements —who doesn't? But after hours of arguing, she wins and I get to have fantastic sex, so in retrospect, I win.

I win because I spend my days with the love of my life. A woman who is not only wonderful but loves me the way I am.

My parents keep asking me when we will get married. I don't have an answer for them. We exchanged our vows a year ago—at Charlie's wedding unbeknownst to our families.

The paper doesn't matter.

I am already spending my life with my best friend and my forever love.

The End

I hope you enjoyed reading Then He Happened, keep reading for an extended excerpt of my bestselling romantic comedy, Maybe Later (Jack and Emmeline's story), My One Regret (my favorite Rockstar Romance) and one of my favorite friends-to-lovers romance, Found.

Acknowledgments

With my less than perfect memory, this tidbit part of the book is yet the most complicated. See, I don't want to forget anyone that's been there for me, but how can I remember all of them when I can barely recall what I did a few hours ago.

So beforehand, my apologies if I missed anyone. Please know that I'm grateful for every person who comes into my life and touches my soul.

First and foremost, I'd like to thank God for all the blessings in my life.

To Luis, who's my Jason at times. A big goof—only for me. Thank you for being the motivating force giving me strength and courage to continue my journey. My tiny ones (who are now adults) Paulina, Andie and Sebastien.

Paulina, thank you so much for everything. This book wouldn't have been possible if it wasn't for her. Seriously.

Ellie McLove who always keeps of with the chaos that happens in my world. Danielle a new addition to the team. I'm so happy to have you on board.

To Hang Le—you complete my books, always. I can't thank you enough for everything you do for me and my stories. Love you my friend.

A million thanks to my team. Without them it'd be difficult to get everything done. Patricia, Yolanda, Michelle, and Melissa.

Kristi, where would I be without you? Thank you for your friendship, your listening ear, your support and for being like a sister.

My amazing ARC team, you ladies rock. Thank you for you patient and support.

To the Book Lovin' Chicas group, thank you so much for your continuous support. For your daily cheers, and the words of encouragement. I'm grateful for you.

Thank you to all the bloggers who help spread the word about my books. Ladies, this release was hard but your messages, your support and friendship kept me going. Though, I guess thank you doesn't cut it, your energy and support are what makes every release a success. Love you all.

To my readers, I am grateful to you. Thank you for reading my words, and for supporting my books. Thank you so much for those emails and notes, they mean so much to me.

All my love,
Claudia

About the Author

Claudia is an award-winning, *USA Today* bestselling author. She lives in Colorado, working for a small IT. She has three children and manages a chaotic household of two confused dogs, and a wonderful husband who shares her love of all things geek. To survive she works continually to find purpose for the voices flitting through her head, plus she consumes high quantities of chocolate to keep the last threads of sanity intact.

To find more about Claudia:
website
Sign up for her newsletter: News Letter
Or come and hang out with her:
Reader group
Goodreads Group

Also By Claudia Burgoa

Standalones

Maybe Later

My One Despair

Knight of Wands

My One Regret

Found

Fervent

Flawed

Until I Fall

Finding My Reason

Christmas in Kentbury

Chaotic Love Duet

Begin with You

Back to You

Unexpected Series

Uncharted

Uncut

Undefeated

Unlike Any Other

Decker the Halls

Made in the USA
Middletown, DE
16 July 2019